TRICKS OF THE TRADE

J. R. ROBERTS

JOVE BOOKS, NEW YORK

THE BERKLEY PUBLISHING GROUP
Published by the Penguin Group
Penguin Group (USA) Inc.
375 Hudson Street, New York, New York 10014, USA
Penguin Group (Canada), 10 Alcorn Avenue, Toronto, Ontario M4V 3B2, Canada
(a division of Pearson Penguin Canada Inc.)
Penguin Books, Ltd. 80 Strand, London WC2R 0RL, England
Penguin Group Ireland, 25 St. Stephen's Green, Dublin 2, Ireland (a division of Penguin Books Ltd.)
Penguin Group (Australia), 250 Camberwell Road, Camberwell, Victoria 3124, Australia
(a division of Pearson Australia Group Pty. Ltd.)
Penguin Books India Pvt. Ltd., 11 Community Centre, Panchsheel Park, New Delhi—110 017, India
Penguin Group (NZ), Cnr. Airborne and Rosedale Roads, Albany, Auckland, New Zealand
(a division of Pearson New Zealand Ltd.)
Penguin Books (South Africa) (Pty.) Ltd., 24 Sturdee Avenue, Rosebank, Johannesburg 2196, South
Africa

Penguin Books Ltd., Registered Offices: 80 Strand, London WC2R 0RL, England

This is a work of fiction. Names, characters, places, and incidents either are the product of the author's imagination or are used fictitiously, and any resemblance to actual persons, living or dead, business establishments, events, or locales is entirely coincidental.

TRICKS OF THE TRADE

A Jove Book / published by arrangement with the author

PRINTING HISTORY
Jove edition / September 2004

ISBN: 0-515-13814-2

JOVE®
Jove Books are published by The Berkley Publishing Group,
a division of Penguin Group (USA) Inc.
375 Hudson Street, New York, New York 10014.
JOVE is a registered trademark of Penguin Group (USA) Inc.
The "J" design is a trademark belonging to Penguin Group (USA) Inc.

PRINTED IN THE UNITED STATES OF AMERICA

10 9 8 7 6 5 4 3 2 1

Thrill of the Kill

Clint stared hard at the older man sitting at the table. "Word is that you were asking about me. I also heard that you planned on shooting someone else if I didn't come find you."

Drogan nodded slowly. "Ah, yes. I must admit that last part was just to get your attention. I know you're not exactly the sort to respond to bad names."

"Well, here I am. Start talking, or I'm walking. What do you want?"

"You feel that?" Drogan asked as he lifted his face as if he were sniffing a fresh, wandering breeze instead of stale smoke. "You feel the blood pumping whenever your hand is set to draw that gun of yours? You feel the tension? It's like lightning."

Clint smiled coldly. "You came here to feel lightning? I suggest you get yourself a woman. They're prettier than me and better for your health."

Suddenly, Drogan's eyes narrowed and he leveled his gaze at Clint as if he was sighting down the barrel of a rifle.

"I came here to kill you, Clint Adams. You can keep talking or defend yourself. It doesn't make a damn bit of difference to me . . ."

ONE

Plattsmith, Ohio, was a town that didn't exactly have deep roots. A place that had been settled less than a decade ago, it prospered by simply being in the right place at the right time. It was a good stopover for folks traveling west, and offered plenty by way of supplies. There was even a railroad line not too far away, which added plenty to the town's prosperity.

As with many towns that grew quickly and catered to folks on the move, Plattsmith had more than its fair share of men who were out to make their fortunes in ways that were somewhat south of honest. They were the types who frequented Plattsmith's many saloons and gaming halls, bragging to all the women they could buy at Felicia's Emporium on Ember Street.

Those men were the ones who tarnished a town's reputation just by being there. On the other hand, nobody was about to ask them to leave because those same men helped line the pockets of more than one undertaker. It wasn't the best arrangement, but it was a common one.

"Clint Adams! Where the hell can I find Clint Adams?"

The man shouting that question at the top of his lungs looked to be in his mid- to late fifties. He was tall and lean, staring out at the world through intense, narrowed eyes. Those eyes were the color of whetstones and glinted with bad intentions.

He'd stepped into the most notorious saloon in town, a place called The Copperhead. To say that the men frequenting The Copperhead were bad sorts would have been a hell of an understatement. As it was, they all glared back at him as though they would just as soon shoot him as speak to him. Many of those looks were turned aside, however, by the venomous stare of the man standing at the door.

Once he could see that he wasn't going to get an answer, the lean older man stepped into the saloon and made his way to the bar. He was dressed in the colors of the night, all black and gray, making his skin tone resemble parched bone. His flesh hung off him as if it was too tired to do much else, creased by imperfections that were the product of long years and hard times.

When he got to the bar, the man slapped his hand flat against the chipped wooden surface and said, "You men deaf or just too damn drunk to answer my question?"

The bartender was a younger man, but had a much softer build than the darkly dressed figure in front of him. Although he tried not to look intimidated by the older man, he didn't do it too convincingly. "What's with all the commotion, old man?" the barkeep asked. "Why don't you have a drink and settle yerself a bit?"

There wasn't anger in the older man's face. Instead, he glared at the barkeep with a menace as genuine as that found in the eyes of the snake that was the saloon's namesake. When he saw the barkeep lower his eyes, the older man said, "I ain't your pappy and if you talk to me like that again, I'll decorate that mirror behind you with the shit that's inside your head."

The older man's hand was on the grip of his holstered

pistol. It had gotten there in a motion that was just a flicker in the barkeep's vision.

Smiling uncomfortably, the barkeep said, "All right. All right. No need for any trouble in here. First drink's on me. How's that?"

"That'll be fine for a start."

Waiting until the drink was in front of him, the older man said, "Now you can answer my first question. Where's Clint Adams?"

"How should I know that?"

"He's in town. My guess is that you either know exactly where he's at or you know someone who does. So which is it?"

The barkeep was getting more nervous by the second. Not only had the older man not made a move toward his free drink, but his hand was still holding firm upon the grip of his pistol. Just then, the barkeep noticed something else. Namely, he saw the reaction of the other men standing at the bar as they watched the old man staring him down. That caused the barkeep to puff out his chest a bit and put some more grit into his voice.

"Take your drink and—"

Before he could get out another word, the barkeep was silenced by a hand that had snapped forward and locked around his throat. That hand belonged to the older man, and had the strength of someone many years his junior.

Without letting go of the barkeep's throat, the older man used his free hand to pick up his drink and tip it into his mouth. He took his time and when the liquor was gone, he calmly set the glass down and then returned his gaze to the barkeep's eyes.

"All right. My drink's gone. Now you've got one more chance to answer my question."

It was too late to salvage any of his pride. The barkeep knew that for damn sure. In fact, the only thing he'd been able to do was toss some more of that pride away on his own. So rather than try to look good in front of his regulars, the barkeep nodded quickly and replied, "Yeah. I'm starting to remember now. Adams was in here."

The older man loosened his grip a bit, but only so the barkeep could pull in a breath. "Go on."

"He came to town a few days ago. Been here every night playing cards. Either here or at the Double Eagle down the road."

"Has he been in today yet?"

"No. Not yet."

The older man thought about that for a moment, started to relax his grip even more, but then suddenly tightened his fist and nearly pulled the barkeep off his feet. "You know where he's staying?"

"N-no. Not for sure. It's either at the Double Eagle or the hotel on Second Avenue. I swear, that's all I know."

"Well, the next time you see him, you tell him Luke Drogan's looking for him. He can either meet up with me or shoot his own self through the skull, because that would be a hell of a lot easier than what I got planned for him."

With that, the older man pushed the barkeep away from him and headed out the door. Seconds later, someone else from inside the saloon followed in his tracks.

TWO

"Hey there!"

Those two words echoed down the street outside The Copperhead Saloon, freezing their intended target in his tracks. The man who'd spoken them was a burly man with a permanent sneer etched onto his rough-hewn features. His thickly muscled arms were covered in dirt and soot, extending like pythons from rolled-up sleeves.

The older man had been crossing the street when he heard the shouted words, and stopped right where he stood. His eyes narrowed into slits and he slowly turned around to face the saloon he'd just left behind.

"You talking to me?"

"Sure I am, old man. What're you askin' around about someone like Clint Adams for?"

"My name's Luke Drogan. What do you care who I'm asking about?"

"Luke Drogan, you say? I thought I recognized you."

"Good. Then you should know to leave me be."

The big man smiled without a bit of humor. His words were filled with a snide, mocking tone. "I heard you were pretty handy with the iron back in your day. Too bad that day is long since gone. You got a hell of a lot of nerve

5

strutting in here like you're still some kind of bad man."

"I didn't come here to prove anything. Especially not to some loud-mouthed kid like yourself."

"Well that's too bad. Because this here loudmouth kid is calling you a washed-up old man who needs to scare bartenders to make himself feel big."

Drogan looked around and noticed the crowd around him was growing by the second. There had been plenty of people in the street before, and even though the numbers had grown, the space around him had also. The bystanders watched the conversation intently, fanning away from both participants with slow, backward steps.

"You're looking for a fight," Drogan said. "Is that it?"

"Nah, but I don't take kindly to some old dog coming into my saloon and talking the way you do. Now that I know who you are, I figure I'd be doing this town a favor by putting a bullet into your sorry carcass. The bounty on yer head ain't too shabby either."

Nodding, Drogan squared off with the younger man and rolled his head from one side to another, working the kinks out with a series of wet snaps. "This really how you want this?"

The younger man looked around at the crowd, which now turned to him in expectation of his reply. All those eyes staring back at him were like hands pushing him further down the road he'd stumbled upon. "Yeah," he said, thinking he didn't really have much of a choice anymore. "That's the way I want it."

"Suit yourself."

With that, Drogan lowered his hand until it was floating over the grip of his pistol. His gun belt was strapped high around the waist beneath a black waistcoat. The gun's grip was plated with polished copper and etched with an intricate design.

The younger man lowered his hand toward his own gun as well, but knew better than to make any more of a reach for the weapon until he was absolutely ready. At that moment, the rest of the street no longer registered in his senses. He couldn't hear the hushed voices or see the eager faces.

All that existed was himself and Drogan.

The older man pulled in a slow, steady breath. Although this was far from his first time facing down a stranger with his very life on the line, he still felt that same twisting in his belly as he had so many years ago. His blood pumped harder through tired veins, and the years that had taken such a heavy toll on his body seemed to melt away.

While the younger man's smile was tense and trembling at the edges, Drogan's was as genuine as a kid's on Christmas morning. Suddenly, the pain in his joints and legs didn't hurt so much. The wheezing in his breath subsided and his hand became steady as a rock.

There was only about five yards separating both men as they stood motionless. A cold, bone-chilling wind slithered down the street like the impatient hand of Death itself. It scraped along the bones of every person lining that street, taking an especially tight grip upon the two figures poised on the brink of destruction.

Nobody knew why those men were about to gun each other down. The truth of the matter was that nobody cared. There was even a hint of confusion behind the younger combatant's eyes as the grim reality of his situation started to sink in.

The only one without a shred of doubt on his face was Drogan. His reasons were known well enough, but only to himself, and he wasn't about to explain himself any further.

It wasn't the time for explanations.

It was the time for action.

The younger man's hand moved first as his will snapped under the pressure of waiting. He reached for his pistol and was thumbing back the hammer before it had even cleared leather.

Drogan reacted instantly, snatching his .44-caliber side arm from its holster without taking his eyes away from the younger man in front of him. Although he drew second, his motions were more fluid than the younger man's and in the blink of an eye, two shots had cracked simultaneously through the air.

Everyone watching the exchange from the sides of the street held their breath. It took them a moment to get over the shock of actual gunfire before their eyes could truly register what had happened.

Both men still stood facing each other, yet neither of them seemed capable of moving. Instead, they just stared at one another, each gripping a pistol with smoke curling from its barrel.

The younger man's eyes drifted up and away from Drogan as though he was looking at something in the sky over the older man's head. But rather than focus on anything in particular, those eyes kept right on going until they'd rolled up into their sockets.

Blood trickled from the younger man's chest, slowly at first, but then started to flow in a crimson splash down the front of his torso. His knees buckled and when he let out a haggard breath, his entire body folded in on itself and dropped to the dirt.

It wasn't until Drogan's body relaxed and he lowered his weapon that the rest of the people surrounding him allowed themselves to move as well. A few women separated from the crowd and rushed over to the young man's body. Even before they got to his side, they could see he was gone. A couple of men walked over to the body, but stood up as soon as they got a look at the young man's dead, unseeing eyes.

When Drogan looked around at the crowd, not one person would meet his eyes. One by one, they looked away from him. Some were unable to hide their fear, and some didn't even bother to try.

Drogan kept his head held high and his shoulders back as he turned away from the corpse he'd created and headed once again in the direction he'd been going before the other man's interruption. As he walked, he looked up toward the same spot that the other man had glanced toward just before he'd died.

It was more of an afterthought really. Having seen so many men gaze up before they passed on, Drogan sometimes wondered if he might catch a glimpse at what they'd seen.

Then again, a part of him knew damn well what those dead men were looking at.

THREE

"Clint Adams?"

The muffled voice could barely be heard. Part of that was because the person doing the talking was trying to do so through a closed, locked door. Another reason for the weakness of that voice was because the speaker wasn't so sure he wanted to be heard.

A spindly little man dressed in a rumpled suit rapped on the door as if he was afraid of touching his knuckles to the wood. His narrow face shifted into a wince as he rapped a little harder and raised his voice just enough to make himself jump.

"Clint Adams? Are you in there?"

Nervously, the little man checked the number on the door for what had to have been the tenth time in as many seconds. Sure enough, just like the previous nine times he'd checked, it was still room number three. According to the register, Clint Adams was supposed to be in room number three.

When he leaned in a little closer, he thought he could even hear some movement behind that door. Still, he couldn't keep from feeling that he was about to get called out for trespassing in the hall of his own hotel. The scrawny man sucked up a deep breath and forced himself to knock one more time, a little harder than he had the other times.

"Mr. Adams?"

Truth be told, he was more than a little relieved when he didn't hear anything from the other side of the door. That way, he could walk away from it with a clear conscience, knowing that he'd done his best.

Of course, there was always the skeleton key that was hanging around his neck.

No. He'd done his best. The scrawny man nodded once to himself with that last thought in mind. After that, he turned around and walked toward the stairs leading back to the lobby . . . quickly.

Inside room number three, Clint hunkered down on his bed with half his face buried in the sheets. He was completely motionless. His eyes were only halfway open, staring toward the door leading out into the hall.

As soon as the knocking stopped and the footsteps in the hall faded away, Clint finally let out the breath he'd been holding. When he did, the sound was caught by a hand that was placed firmly against his mouth.

"I thought he was going to stand out there pounding on that door forever," Clint said after pulling the hand away from his face.

He tried to get up, but there was something holding him down. Since that certain something was a buxom blonde wearing nothing but a white lace choker, he didn't exactly mind that particular weight on his back. It had been her hand that was clamped over Clint's mouth, which was why he hadn't minded it one bit.

"And I thought you were about to get up and answer that damn door," the blonde replied.

"What if it was something important, Amanda? I think I may have heard shots a minute ago."

The blonde lifted herself up just enough for Clint to roll onto his back. From there, she sat down on top of him, straddling his waist and shaking her long hair back over her shoulders. "There's shooting every other night around here. Besides, what could be more important than being right here, right now, with me?"

Clint looked up at her and let his eyes wander slowly over the ample curves of her breasts and hips. Her deep blue eyes were vivid even in the flickering light of the room's single lantern. Her large nipples were becoming erect just by him looking at her as his hands drifted ever closer.

"When you look at me like that," he said, "it makes me feel like I couldn't go anywhere else even if I'd wanted to."

Smiling, she closed her eyes and leaned her head back slightly. "Oh, yeah?" she said, placing her hands over his and running them over her breasts, down her stomach, and back up again. "And what about now?"

"Now, I'm wondering why the hell I'd want to go anywhere else in the first place."

Amanda said nothing in response to that. Instead, she let her actions speak for her as she began to slowly grind against Clint's body using nothing but her hips. She spread her legs open a bit so the lips of her vagina could slide along the shaft of his growing erection.

The more she ground her hips back and forth, the wetter she became. And the more she rubbed those moist lips against him, the harder Clint got.

"Nobody's taking you from me, Clint. Not for now anyway. Not that little man that runs this hotel and not whatever it was he wanted to see you about." Pressing her hands flat against Clint's chest, Amanda shifted herself until she felt the tip of his cock push inside her.

"You're all mine," she purred, lowering herself down,

slowly taking him completely inside. "You're not going anywhere."

Clint smiled and shifted his hips beneath her. With a gentle push up at the right moment, he penetrated her even deeper, causing Amanda to take in a deep, satisfied breath.

"You see me trying to escape?" he asked.

Amanda's skin was hot to the touch and soft beneath his hands. She smelled like rose water with a hint of powder, which made him want to press his own naked body against her even more. As if sensing this desire inside him, Amanda lowered herself so her face was directly above Clint's. Her hair fell down to create a soft curtain around them both.

"I wonder what he wanted," she said, giving a short, sideways glace toward the door.

Clint moved both his hands along her body, brushing against her sides and coming to a rest upon her firm, ample buttocks. Squeezing her contoured flesh, he pulled her forward while pumping his hips up at the same time.

"I don't care what he wanted," Clint said, guiding her body back and forth as he drove up into her. "All I know right now is what *I* want."

FOUR

After burying his cock deep inside her, Clint slid his hands up over her back and wrapped his arms around Amanda's body to hold her tight. She melted into his embrace, kissing him wherever she could reach, allowing her tongue to flick out and sample his neck, ear, and shoulder.

She hardly even seemed to notice that Clint was moving both of them over onto the other side of the mattress until her side bumped against the soft blankets. Amanda's eyes shot wide open and she let out a surprised gasp as she was tossed onto her back so Clint could climb on top of her.

Clint's breaths were growing deeper, and every inhale pulled Amanda's sweet scent deep into his lungs. He could feel the primal part of himself stirring at the sight of her naked body beneath him. Amanda's chest was heaving, her head was tossed back, and her legs were spread open wide to receive him. All of that made Clint forget about any part of the world that didn't involve her.

He only wanted to taste her.

Only wanted to feel her pressed against him.

Only wanted to be inside her once again.

All that remained now was to reach out and take what

14

he wanted the most. And so, closing both of his hands around Amanda's, he did exactly that.

Clint settled in between her legs and shifted his weight until he could feel the tip of his cock sliding against the wet lips of her pussy. Amanda reached down to take hold of his penis and guide it into her, letting out a prolonged sigh as he drove it in as far as he could go.

Feeling her body envelop him made Clint feel relieved as well. He'd wanted her so badly that it would have hurt to deny himself any longer. That was the way he'd felt when he'd first laid eyes on her, and ever since then, he'd been thinking about nothing but what he wanted to do once he got her alone.

That time had come and he wasn't about to waste a second of it. Propping himself up with one hand, Clint ran his other hand over Amanda's side, feeling the way her hips shifted back and forth as he pumped in and out of her and tracing a line all the way up to her breasts. Their smooth curves swayed with the rhythm of Clint and Amanda's bodies. The large, dark nipples became more erect beneath the subtle touch of his hand.

When he pushed into her one more time, Clint situated himself so that he was upright and kneeling between her legs. He had one hand on each of her thighs and massaged the muscles there as he began to thrust into her with renewed vigor.

Every time his body would push against her, Clint heard Amanda let out a gasp of pleasure. Each time, that gasp would become more powerful, as if she was the one driving him to pump into her harder and harder every time.

Finally, Amanda arched her back against the bed and started moaning loudly as she let go of any last bit of restraint inside her. Clint took that as a cue as well, and allowed himself to hand the reins over to that primal part inside him that only wanted to make the pleasure he was feeling grow and grow.

Amanda's fingernails raked over his skin and her groans became almost primal as well. When Clint took hold of her hips and lifted her off the bed so he could pull her toward him as he thrust his hips forward, she reached behind her to dig her nails into the pillow as if she was holding on for dear life.

The sheer power of their passion caused Amanda's climax to rush in upon her. The orgasm swelled inside her, causing her to take a deep breath and hold it until the tickle between her legs grew into a full explosion of pleasure. When it came, she bit down on her lip and snaked her fingers through her hair.

Clint could feel the lips between her legs tightening around his cock as well as the tremble that worked its way throughout her entire body. When he slid in and out of her now, she was even tighter than before. The feel of those tight, wet lips gripping him made his own climax speed its way through his system.

He could feel her body tensing in anticipation of the final push of her orgasm. Clint slowed his pace down to a gentle motion so he could prolong the moment, which he never wanted to end. He let his eyes wander over her sweaty body.

Amanda's breasts glistened with perspiration. Her muscles were tense and jumping beneath her skin. Even the way she turned her head and writhed in the grip of her orgasm made Clint grow harder between her legs.

As if he was being led by sheer animal instinct, Clint dropped down on top of her, grabbed hold of her hands, and pinned them to the bed. Their eyes locked and he started to thrust powerfully into her. His motion and strength caused Amanda's breath to catch in her throat until her final climax caused her eyes to clamp shut beneath the sheer force of it.

Clint felt his own climax building inside him and did nothing to stop it. When it came, it washed over him like a tidal wave, forcing his hands to tighten around Amanda's until he had to force himself to let go before hurting her.

When nothing more remained from either of their orgasms except for a faint tickle, they both opened their eyes and looked at each other. Clint lifted himself up and kneeled once more on the bed. He ran both hands over his face and when he took them away, he found Amanda still staring at him with wide, excited eyes.

It seemed as though both of them wanted to talk, but neither had the strength. Instead, Clint dropped down onto the bed beside her and rubbed his hand over her shoulder as she draped her naked body across his chest.

Like the tapping of mice behind a loose board, there suddenly came another series of knocks from the door leading out to the hallway.

"Clint Adams," came the all-too-familiar voice. "Mr. Adams, I uh . . . I know you're in there."

Amanda looked at him like a little girl who'd been caught trying to steal candy. Apparently, Clint had a similar expression on his face because they both broke into a fit of laughter that could barely even be held back.

FIVE

When the door to room number three finally opened, the skinny man outside was greeted by a disheveled Clint Adams, who didn't look at all happy to be away from his bed. His hair was a dark mop on top of his head, but Clint's eyes still retained their sharpness. Every move he made was short and to the point, much like his voice.

"What do you want?" Clint asked.

Even though he'd been waiting for this conversation for what seemed like hours, the skinny man who'd been knocking on the door came up short when put on the spot. He started to stammer out a few words, but stopped himself so he could say something more intelligible.

"You . . . uh . . . someone's been asking around for you," was the best the scrawny man could do on short notice.

Clint's brows furrowed and he thought about anyone who might know he was in town. On the other hand, this surely wouldn't be the first time that others had known where he was without his knowledge. Shrugging, he said, "Who's been asking?"

"I . . . uhhh . . . don't rightly know."

That caused Clint's brows to furrow even more. This

time, the sharpness in his eyes was tempered by no small amount of anger. "Well, thanks for delivering that bit of news. If that's all, I've got better things to do right now."

As he heard that, the skinny man was just able to get a glimpse at the blonde reclining on Clint's bed. She stretched her back and looked over toward the door without making any attempt to cover her nakedness. When she spotted the man staring at her from the hall, she simply waved.

"I can see that you've got your hands full," the skinny man said in a quickening tone. "But I thought you'd want to know about this as soon as possible. The gentleman asking for you has been quite . . . ahh . . . vocal about wanting to find you."

Clint stopped just short of closing the door on the smaller man's face. Just then, he recalled the noises he'd heard from outside not too long ago. "How vocal?"

"He was insistent enough to get someone to run down here and beg me to fetch you. Apparently, this man is the violent type, and I believe there may already have been an incident to that effect."

"Is that what that shooting was about?"

"I'm not sure, but I would assume that—"

He was cut off by the sudden slamming of the door. It hit the frame with a jarring thump, soon to be followed by the thumping of heavy footsteps coming from the room itself. Although the skinny fellow had definitely noticed the aggravated look on Clint's face, he still remained where he was so he could listen to the series of noises coming from behind the closed door.

There were a few words spoken back and forth between Clint and Amanda, but the skinny man couldn't make out any specifics from where he was standing. He did hear enough, however, to piece together the general flow of what was being said.

Clint wasn't happy. That was for sure.

As for the woman, it sounded as though she was confused at first, and then became more annoyed as the stomping went on.

Finally, just when the skinny man couldn't decide on whether he should try knocking again or just walk away, the door swung open in front of him. Even though he couldn't see the expression on his own face, the scrawny fellow could feel the surprise etched upon his features.

If he'd been in a better mood, Clint would have found the gaping look on the other man's face amusing. As it was, he was anything but amused. Amanda had been upset that she didn't get another tussle beneath the sheets with him, and Clint was feeling pretty much the same way. In fact, it had taken every shred of willpower he had to pull his clothes on, open the door, and step outside.

"All right," Clint said as he pulled the door shut behind him. "This had better be good."

Now that he was dressed and had something separating himself from the sight and scent of the beautiful naked blonde in his room, Clint recognized the skinny man as the clerk from the hotel lobby. Of course, the man looked a lot different than when he'd handed Clint his key. For one thing, there hadn't been so much sweat on his brow when the skinny man was behind his desk.

The fact that he was moving again seemed to have a good effect on the clerk, and his voice steadied the closer he got to the top of the stairs. "I assure you, Mr. Adams, I wouldn't have pulled you away from ... uh ... well your room unless I thought it was important."

"So this is about a shooting?"

"Maybe. I-I was hoping you might know some more about this than I do."

"Now why would I know more about it?" Clint asked, only then buttoning the top button of his shirt. "I've been busy."

"Yes, I heard."

Clint saw the clerk sneak a glance over his shoulder toward him, but the skinny fellow knew better than to meet Clint's stare. He surely wouldn't have liked the nasty look that was on Clint's face after hearing that last sentence.

"Well, since your ears are so good," Clint said, "you'll hear me just fine when I tell you to get to the point of you dragging me out here."

That seemed to light a fire under the hotel clerk, and suddenly the skinny man couldn't talk fast enough. "I heard someone was looking for you who appeared to be some kind of gunman. It was only mentioned in passing, and I didn't think much of it until I heard the shooting."

"Whoever was shooting was the same one looking for me?"

"I didn't know that at first, but then I got word from someone else that it was the same man. I still didn't want to disturb you for . . . uhh . . . obvious reasons, but then I got another message. This came from someone who overheard it from the source itself."

"Source? What source?"

"This gunman. He said that if he didn't find you, he'd just have to take on anyone else foolish enough to face him until you found your way to the street." Seeing the look on Clint's face, the clerk added, "His words, not mine."

Letting out an aggravated sigh, Clint tried not to think about what was still waiting for him up in his room, and shoved his arms through the sleeves of the jacket he'd been carrying. As much as he wanted to keep his spot warm next to Amanda, it didn't sit right with Clint to have some loudmouth gunslinger hurting random targets just to get under his skin.

"Where was all this shooting happening?" Clint asked.

"Outside of The Copperhead Saloon."

"Anything else you can tell me before I head over there?"

"Just that whoever is causing all that commotion is handy with iron. He killed Pete Rowlands like he was nothing, and Pete's not too shabby himself."

"All right then. I'll go have a look for myself before anyone else tries to step up and take this fellow on himself. A man with that big of a mouth probably won't have to wait long before someone tries to shut him up. And do me a favor, will you?"

"Sure. That is . . . I'll do my best."

"Make sure the law's on their way over there."

The clerk nodded. "And what about the lady in your room? Should I give her a message from you?"

"Yeah. Tell her I'll be right back."

SIX

Clint hadn't made it more than ten steps outside the front door of the hotel before he knew his promise to Amanda would be hard to keep. The Copperhead wasn't far from the hotel, and there was already plenty of commotion as people rushed up and down the street in a flurry of excitement.

Everyone was chattering amongst themselves, and most of the talk involved the shooting. After hearing all the whispers and feeling the tension in the air, Clint felt as though he was getting wrapped up in the ruckus himself. It wasn't hard to do since the night seemed to be taking on a wildness of its own that grew like a fire that was spreading from one stack of dry kindling to another.

Clint turned the corner off Second Avenue and headed for The Copperhead, which was a little more than halfway down the block. It was plain to see that that particular saloon was the eye of this hurricane. The streets outside were crowded, and the doors leading into the establishment were constantly swinging open and closed with a steady flow of foot traffic. What set the scene apart from any other circus was the sight just outside The Copperhead's doors.

In the street, like a sobering jolt to the system, was a splash of thick dark liquid in the dirt. In the moonlight, it looked black as tar, but Clint recognized it immediately as blood. A somewhat closer look revealed the indents where the body had been lying, as well as the twin tracks created by a set of heels being dragged through the dirt.

When he looked up from the grisly sight, Clint swore he could taste the bitter sting of gunpowder in the back of his throat. It tasted like death itself was still hanging in the air looking down on that street.

With his mind set firmly on the task at hand, Clint turned his back on the bloodstained street and walked up to the front door of the saloon. Like many of the rougher establishments he'd seen, The Copperhead used a pair of batwing doors as an entrance. Those flapping doors weren't normal for any business that ever wanted to lock up on occasion, but were more economical in places that had folks being tossed out on a regular basis. Clint stepped through the swinging doors, and kept walking before they swatted him on his back as they closed.

The inside of The Copperhead was twice as chaotic as the outside. Judging by the rowdy voices, bawdy laughter, and occasional scream, one might think that a shooting was the largest boon to business the place had ever had. Even so, there was still plenty of space for Clint to maneuver and he made his way to the bar. Made out of wood that had more chips in it than a broken set of teeth, the bar was covered with water stains and darker ones that were reminiscent of the one in the street outside. Clint didn't even want to think about what caused the gritty feel beneath his boot when he set it upon the rail.

No matter how crowded it was, the bartender spotted Clint without much trouble at all. "What're you drinkin', stranger?"

"I'll have a beer."

The keg wasn't too far away and before too long at

all, a dirty glass filled with a foamy, murky liquid was set on top of the bar. Clint picked it up, felt that the stuff was warmer than piss, and took a tentative sip. The beer didn't quite taste like piss, but it was close enough.

Beaming proudly despite the sour look on Clint's face, the bartender said, "If it's cards yer after, I can steer you toward a good game. If you got a hankering for some female companionship, there's plenty of them around here as well."

"Actually, I'm looking for someone in particular."

A greedy smile came onto the barkeep's face and he leaned forward to put both elbows on the table. "Really? Tell me who you're after and I'll see what I can do. Of course, any donation you might offer could help jostle my memory."

"I don't have a name, but the man I'm after was just involved in a shooting."

"There were two men in that shooting, stranger. Which one you interested in?"

"The one that lived. I hear he's been asking around about me."

"Yeah?" The barkeep lost the glint in his eyes and his entire expression became more cautious. "And who might you be?"

"Clint Adams."

More often than not, Clint preferred not to have everyone know exactly who he was. Especially in places filled with gun hands trying to make a name for themselves, tossing around any name well known in those circles was just asking for trouble. Sometimes, however, it was simply the shortest line between two points.

"He was asking about you," the barkeep said after pushing himself away from the bar and taking a step back. "Right over there. That table in the back."

Clint looked in the direction the barkeep had mentioned, but couldn't see much more than a few shapes through the milling crowd. Slapping some money onto the bar, Clint left the beer behind and made his way toward the back of the saloon.

More than once, he had to dodge someone who'd been pushed in his direction, or even catch someone else before they fell directly in front of him. The stink of stale liquor and cigar smoke filled the air. By the time he made it to the back of the room, Clint felt as if he had to fight to take a breath that wasn't a struggle to keep down.

"Are you the one looking for me?" Clint asked the man sitting at a table in the back of the saloon.

The man looked big sitting down, and when he got up, he was nothing less than a mountain. His face was covered by a thick, tangled beard as well as an ugly assortment of scars. A loud, booming voice echoed from behind that beard when the big man let out a snarling laugh and walked away.

Nodding and trying to fight back the thoughts of what he could be doing now instead of walking through some smelly saloon, Clint spotted a table that was so far in the shadows that he'd overlooked it the first time. Sitting at that table was an older fellow calmly smoking a cigar and watching Clint with calm, dark eyes.

Despite the shadows, Clint knew that older man was the one he was after. The specter of death still seemed to be hanging over his shoulder.

SEVEN

"Don't bother sitting down, Adams," the older man said through teeth still clenched around his cigar. "I came here to face you in the street."

"You have me at a disadvantage. I don't know your name, but you seem to know me well enough."

"Plenty of folks know about you. I doubt you've heard much about me."

"Why don't I be the judge of that?"

"All right then," the older man said before taking the cigar from his mouth and flicking the ashes onto the floor. "My name's Luke Drogan."

Clint's smile came more as a reflex than anything else. "Luke Drogan? You mean Two-Cent Drogan?"

Drogan's eyebrow raised slightly, which was as expressive as he was about to allow himself to be under the circumstances. "You've heard the name?"

"Sure, but I also heard you were dead."

"I've heard that one myself. Until recently, I thought it best to let the rumor circulate so I could get some peace and quiet. I'm sure you know how it feels to have someone dogging your trail for one reason or another."

"Damn right, I do. That's the reason why I'm here and

not back in my hotel room tiring myself out with a very energetic blonde. There's one thing I heard about you that's always sparked my interest."

Drogan stood and shifted his feet so that his holster was slightly closer to his gun hand. "Let me guess. You want to know if it really was me who shot his way out of that fort in Wyoming?"

"No, not that. Your namesake. You still carrying it with you?"

The older man's scowl lifted somewhat, and he cocked his head as though he was regarding Clint in a different light. "Figures you'd be more interested in that, I guess," he said, lifting his hand toward his firearm. "What with you being The Gunsmith and all. Here. Take a look for yourself."

When Drogan's hand touched his pistol, it was with a deliberately slow movement. Even after he started lifting it from its holster, he made sure to keep his thumb away from the hammer and his finger along the bottom of the cylinder instead of on top of the trigger.

Clint watched Drogan carefully. Although he didn't make a move toward his own pistol, he was ready to draw and fire the modified Colt at a moment's notice.

But as Clint looked into the other man's eyes, he knew that moment wasn't going to come. Well, it wouldn't come just then anyway.

Keeping his movements slow and deliberate, Drogan drew his weapon and held it at hip level in front of him. At first, he trained the barrel on Clint and glared at him as if he meant to fire. Before the moment could become too tense, however, he opened his fingers slightly and held the gun so Clint could get a look at the ornately decorated handle.

Out of all the gunfighters that Clint had heard about over the years, Luke Drogan had stood out in his mind because of one thing. The gun Clint was now looking at was supposedly crafted by a master gunsmith from Wales, and there hadn't been another one like it made since.

That gun was also the source of Drogan's nickname. He was called Two-Cent Drogan because the handle of his gun was plated in copper and engraved with the likeness of an enlarged penny. One side of the grip was heads and the other was tails. Each side was more of a work of art instead of just an accurate depiction of a U.S. coin.

Clint soaked up the sight of it while trying to keep track of Drogan's movements as well. After all, Clint was there because the older man wanted to shoot him down, but it was still awfully hard to take his eyes away from the breathtaking craftsmanship that had gone into that gun.

Only another gunsmith could have appreciated the way the copper was perfectly blended into the body of the pistol. Even the engraving melded into the entire weapon in the same way wood grain was a part of the entire tree.

"That's a fine piece of iron you've got there," Clint said with genuine admiration. "Mind if I take a closer look?"

Drogan's fingers tightened around the grip once more and he holstered it with a quick spinning flourish. "I'll extend you the courtesy of a gander, but don't take me for a fool."

"I'm not the sort that has to gun down unarmed men."

"And I'm not the sort that likes to be unarmed."

Clint shrugged and nodded once. "Fair enough. So were you the one that shot down some kid in front of this place to get my attention?"

"I put a smart-mouthed asshole out of his misery, but it wasn't entirely to get your attention. Places like this are filled with the kind of trash that would rather kill than carry a conversation."

"So they are," Clint said, fixing his eyes firmly upon the older man in front of him. "Shouldn't you be a little more concerned with the law coming for you?"

Drogan looked around and said, "These cowboys don't care if we kill each other and neither does the law. Besides, it was a fair fight. Anyone in here will tell you the same."

"Fair maybe. But that doesn't mean there was a real point to it. Word got back to me that you were asking about me. I also heard that you planned on shooting someone else if I didn't come find you."

"Ah, yes. Well, I must admit that last part was just to get your attention. I know you're not exactly the type to respond to bad names."

"Well, either way, here I am. Start saying something I want to hear, or I'll be walking back to my room. What do you want?"

"You feel that?" Drogan asked as he lifted his face as if he was sniffing a fresh, wandering breeze instead of stale smoke. "You feel the blood pumping whenever your hand is set to draw that gun of yours? You feel the tension? It's like lightning."

"You came here to feel lightning? I suggest you get yourself a woman. They're prettier than me and better for your health."

Suddenly, Drogan's eyes narrowed and he leveled his gaze at Clint as if he was sighting down the barrel of a rifle. "I came here to kill you, Clint Adams. You can keep talking or defend yourself. It doesn't make a damn bit of difference to me."

EIGHT

Clint had heard a whole lot of bluffs in his time. He'd been bluffed in the biggest games by the best players out there and in the process, he'd gotten to know a bluff when he heard one.

Luke Drogan wasn't bluffing.

Clint would have staked his life on it. And if he didn't do something pretty quickly to defuse the situation, he figured he might just lose that very thing.

"You don't want to do this, Drogan," Clint said. There was no mistaking the menace in Clint's voice. It was as thick as the venom running through a snake's fangs and every bit as real.

The older man was lean and his face was gaunt. Despite those things, he looked to be anything but sickly. His eyes were sharp as any man half his age, and his hand was steady as a rock with his famous gun wrapped within its grasp.

"This is how it's going to go," Drogan announced. "We're both going outside and then we're settling this."

"But there's nothing to settle! I've never even met you until just a couple minutes ago." Clint didn't have to look around to see that everyone nearby was staring at him.

31

He could feel the thirst for blood like a chilling fog hanging in the air. "You're crazy. Is that it? I wouldn't have guessed it, but that's the only explanation for what you're doing."

"I don't need to explain myself to you, Adams. All you need to know is that I mean to kill you. Telling you that much was a courtesy on my part, so don't throw it in my face."

Clint stood and stared at the other man, ignoring everyone that was staring at him. He was watching closely enough to be able to spot the first move Drogan made toward taking a shot at him, so that didn't concern him. What did bother him was the oddity of this whole situation.

As he studied Drogan, Clint scoured through his memories for any trace of bad blood between himself and Two-Cent. Even though he'd been forced to kill plenty of men, Clint didn't have any trouble recalling any of their faces. Most of the time, trying to put them out of his mind was the tricky part.

He scoured his past for a few more moments, but still came up short when it came to anything that would connect him to Drogan. "Look here, Drogan. If I wronged you somehow, just tell me about it. Maybe there's been some kind of a mistake."

"The only mistake I see here is when I figured you'd be man enough to take me up on my challenge."

A hush went through the crowd that had gathered around Drogan and Clint like a ripple traveling over the surface of a pond. Not only did Clint feel it himself, but he knew it would be coming even before Drogan had finished his sentence. The plain fact of the matter was that the dogs who spent their lives in places like The Copperhead lived for moments just like this one.

Plenty of them died after those same moments.

Clint had yet to take his eyes off the older man. He'd

spent this entire time gathering everything he could learn about Drogan by just looking him in the eye and listening to the tone of his voice. He had yet to come up with a real reason for the challenge that had been given, but Clint had learned something else.

"I don't want to kill you tonight, Drogan," Clint said, taking a step back. "And you don't want to die. I can see that just as plain as the nose on your face."

Drogan shook his head slowly. "Don't test me, Adams."

"I'm not testing you, but I'm also sick of talking to you."

"Draw that gun, Adams, or so help me . . ."

"Have some of the beer, Drogan. That stuff may just be foul enough to give you the punishment you're after."

"Adams, goddammit!"

Clint didn't say another word. Instead, he tipped his hat and then turned his back on Drogan completely so he could walk toward the door.

Although there was some confusion on the faces that Clint saw as he walked out of that saloon, what he saw mostly was disappointment. Coming from men who would rather watch men kill each other for their own enjoyment, it truly didn't surprise Clint. But he wasn't there to entertain those drunkards like some kind of barroom gladiator, so he kept walking and nobody was man enough to stop him.

Nobody, that is, except for the one man who'd dragged Clint out of his room with threats of violence.

"My promise still stands, Adams," Drogan shouted. "If I can't take you on, then I'll take on anyone here."

"That's your prerogative," Clint said without looking back. "I don't want any part of this nonsense."

"Nonsense?" That one whispered word drifted through the chaos in the room like a dagger sliding through layers of protective clothing to sink into its target.

Clint heard the word, and although he didn't break his stride, he kept every one of his senses on the lookout for whatever might come next.

"Nonsense?" Drogan hissed again. "You think this is nonsense?"

The thump of the older man's footsteps came up behind him, but Clint acted as though he wasn't even aware of them. Once he stepped outside, Clint stepped all the way to the edge of the boardwalk before spinning around on the balls of his feet and lowering his gun hand to the grip of his Colt. "You want to die, Drogan? Then you can wait around for old age to take you or let someone else do the job. I'm not interested. And I won't be threatened either, so you can hold your tongue because I'm not in the mood for that bullshit either."

Drogan had stopped just outside the door to The Copperhead and was poised with his gun ready to draw. "Step out into the street and say that to me."

Clint didn't know which struck him as more ridiculous: the fact that Drogan was still trying to bait him, or the fact that he'd let himself be lured into the saloon in the first place. One thing he knew for damn sure was that he wasn't about to give the older man anything he wanted.

"You want to dance in the street so badly?" Clint said. "I'm sure you'll find someone here to take you up on the offer. Hell, gun them all down. If they play whatever game this is you're running, then they've got it coming."

Nodding once and squaring his shoulders, Drogan said, "All right then, Adams. If this is the only way, then this is the way it's got to be."

With that, the older man drew in a breath and steeled himself. Clint recognized the tensing of the other man's muscles and the way his eyes had glazed over like a sheet of ice sweeping across the top of a lake.

Drogan was about to draw.

He was truly about to stand there and take a shot at Clint for no good reason.

"I would've expected this from some punk kid trying to prove themselves," Clint said. "But not from a man who's been in this way of life for as long as you and I have. You've got nothing to prove. Not to me."

"Does that mean you're backing down?"

"If that's how you want to look at it, then sure. I'll back down. I've seen too much blood in my time to spill more over something as bizarre as this."

And with that, Clint took one more look into Drogan's eyes. There was a change beneath the older man's surface and as soon as Clint spotted it, he turned his back on him for the final time that night and walked away down the length of the boardwalk.

NINE

It was one of the longest walks Clint had taken for some time. Every step of the way, he half-expected to hear the crack of gunfire followed by a stabbing pain in his back. After that, his imagination ran wild and not anywhere close to a good direction.

What kept him moving was what he'd seen in Drogan's eyes just before he'd left. Clint had been certain the older man was preparing to fire, but that had changed at the last second once Clint had made it clear he was leaving anyway. It all boiled down to the fact that Clint was simply tired of going back and forth with Drogan.

Clint stuck to the boardwalk for a simple, somewhat petty reason. That seemed to be where Drogan didn't want him to go. On a childish level, Clint got a kick from walking those boards, even though he thought he might get shot in the back for doing so. But Clint's instincts proved themselves once again and no shot was fired into his back.

When he got back to the hotel, Clint walked straight up to his room. Amanda was still there, except she'd gotten herself dressed and looked as though she was seconds away from leaving. Clint went straight for the window of his room and pulled open the curtains.

The windows started at the floor and were almost as tall as he was. They pulled open and led out to a narrow balcony overlooking Second Avenue. Clint squeezed through the narrow opening, dragging a chair out with him.

"In case you haven't noticed," Amanda said. "I'm still here."

Before sitting on the chair he'd brought outside, Clint went back to the blonde and wrapped his arms around her. He didn't say a word before pressing his lips against hers and holding her tight as he kissed her with passion that surprised even him. When he pulled back, he heard her pull in a deep, gasping breath.

Amanda's eyes were wide and her smile was full of surprise. "Well, that's better!"

"I missed you while I was gone." Clint's hands roamed over her body, feeling the smooth, familiar curves of her hips and buttocks through the material of her dress.

"Not that I'm complaining," she said, "but it was only about half an hour or so, wasn't it? Either that or I fell asleep."

"No, you're right. It just seems like a lot longer than that. Want to sit outside with me?"

"Not just yet." With that, Amanda went in for another kiss, and this time she let her tongue flicker across his lips and pressed her hips against Clint's body. Although she could feel him responding to her, she could still see in his eyes that something was troubling him. "What's wrong?"

"Actually, I'm feeling a lot better now."

"Then what happened while you were out?"

Smiling, Clint tried to think of a way to phrase it, but came up short. "You know something? I'm not really sure what happened."

Amanda let him go and grabbed the second chair from inside the room. "Come on," she said, pushing Clint toward the balcony while taking her own chair outside as well. "Have a seat and tell me all about it."

Clint had met Amanda sometime ago, and their paths just seemed to cross every so often. She had the hankering to travel almost as much as he did, and when they met up again, the spark that was always between them never failed to ignite. Still, because of the danger surrounding his life, Clint was reluctant to drag anyone else too far into it. Sometimes, that could prove fatal.

Without delving too deeply, Clint told her the basics. After all, it felt good to get it in the open just so he could get a fresh look at it himself. Also, what he told her had been witnessed by everyone who'd wanted to watch what happened inside The Copperhead.

Unfortunately, even after telling what had gone on at that saloon, Clint was still confused.

"Sounds to me like he was just picking a fight," Amanda said. "There's plenty of men like that around here, especially in that filthy saloon. I thought you get a lot of men coming after you like that."

"I do," Clint replied. "But not men like Two-Cent Drogan. He's a higher caliber than the dregs that just want to spread their name around. He's already got a name for himself."

"Maybe he just wants to make a bigger name." Shrugging, Amanda added, "I haven't heard of him."

"This whole thing just goes against the grain somehow. It didn't seem right at the time, and the more I think about it, the more wrong it feels. Drogan went through a lot of trouble to call me out when there are plenty of targets at The Copperhead for someone just looking to rack up some kills."

Amanda reached out to rub her hand along Clint's shoulder. "You're more than just another kill for some gunfighter. You'd be the kill of a lifetime."

"Maybe. I don't know." Clint knew he wasn't going to find out exactly what was so bothersome about his confrontation with Drogan. It was like a name that drifted on the edge of his mind, and the more he tried to put his finger on it, the farther away it flew. Rather than trying some more to catch it, Clint looked at the street below and watched the occasional people passing by.

Amanda had already moved behind him and was massaging his shoulders. "You know what you need?" she whispered in a voice that went straight to the knot in Clint's muscles and worked it free. "You need to just relax and give yourself a moment to think. Whatever the problem is with this other gunfighter, it sounds like something that doesn't concern you."

"He wants to kill me, Amanda. I'd say that concerns me."

"But you're so busy wondering about the whys and what-fors when your part is done. He didn't kill you and you didn't kill him. You're not even in that saloon anymore, so for now anyway, you're done with it and him."

"You know something? You're absolutely right." Clint swiveled in his chair so he could reach around and get hold of Amanda. Once he had his hands on her waist, he drew her over the arm of the chair, off her feet, and onto his lap. She landed with a gasp, but settled easily against him.

Running his fingers through her hair, Clint said, "The whole time I was over there, I couldn't stop thinking about how much I would rather be back here with you. And then once I do get back here, I keep thinking about what happened at the saloon.

"You're right, Amanda. It's over for now and I'm back here right where I wanted to be. Drogan's probably just got something in his craw about taking me on and drank too much while he was thinking about it. Whatever the reason, I don't care."

"Is that so?"

"Yeah. That's so."

Amanda wrapped one arm around Clint's neck and pulled him closer so she could run her tongue along the edge of his ear and nibble his earlobe enticingly. "Prove it," she whispered.

Clint slid one arm under Amanda's legs and placed the other across her back. From there, he stood up and picked her up right along with him. The kissing on his neck and ear didn't stop. In fact, he could hear her breathing quicken as he lifted her up, and become even heavier as he carried her back into the room and onto the bed.

She didn't let go of him as he set her down. Without taking her hands away from him, she slid her fingers under his shirt and pulled it roughly off him. Clint pulled her skirt up so he could enter her the moment she unbuttoned his pants.

Not even halfway undressed, he slid his cock inside her and found Amanda's pussy to be dripping with anticipation. Once he was inside her, The Copperhead and Luke Two-Cent Drogan couldn't have been further from his mind.

TEN

For Luke Drogan, life itself hadn't started until he'd killed his first man. On that day, when he was fourteen years old, his entire world had come into focus for the first time. Before that, everything had only been doing what he was told and taking whatever pleasure he could while dodging his father's fists.

Drogan didn't consider his childhood to be particularly bad. It was just not much of anything in his mind. Nothing special enough to bother remembering. But when he was fourteen and he'd found himself with someone else's gun in his hands and his finger on the trigger, Drogan felt as though he was seeing everything through another set of eyes.

To this day, he couldn't recall what that other kid's name was. All he remembered was that the kid at the other end of that stolen gun was a few years older than him and had just spent the last several hours calling him every rotten name he could think of.

The youthful Drogan had turned his back on the other boy, and was about to start running away when he noticed something wedged in the belt of one of the others standing nearby. It was a gun, and when Drogan had set his sights on it, there was no stopping him until he got that firearm in his eager little fists.

Thinking back on it, he didn't even really know how he'd wrangled that gun away from its owner. He was the smallest kid there, which was why he'd become the butt of so many jokes. He did recall the other fella hadn't given the gun up voluntarily, but had given it up all the same.

Drogan did remember his hands aching when he finally got to the gun, but all that pain disappeared the moment he felt his fingers clench tightly around that grip. The iron was heavy and rusted, but it felt like polished gold to him. He could still hear that first grating clack as he'd pulled the hammer back the way he'd seen his father do once or twice before.

Even when he'd gotten that gun in his hands and turned around to face his tormentor, Drogan still had to withstand the barrage of profanities being thrown at him. He might have forgotten the kid's name, but Drogan would never forget how incessantly that bastard had made fun of him.

Day after day, month after month, the boy had sunk his teeth into Drogan, starting from the moment his family had settled in the area, and would never let him loose. Drogan had wondered why someone would treat him like that when they didn't even know him. His father just told him that the world was a hard place and he might as well start getting used to it.

Well, he had gotten used to it, but it was the way a dog got used to being beaten. And if he wasn't being prodded and harassed by that asshole kid, Drogan was being swatted and kicked by his own father. All of this had led up to that day when he was fourteen and something inside him had driven him to wrench that gun away from the kid wearing it.

That moment, more than any other from his early

years, was clear as crystal in Drogan's head. Besides the sublime feel of the clunky weapon in his hands, he could remember the face of that asshole fucker who'd made so many days of his youth a hellish struggle.

At first, that other boy had been making fun of him as always. Still calling him names and stringing together as many profanities as his little brain could come up with. Even when he saw that Drogan had armed himself, that prick kept on making fun of him.

"What're you gonna do with that, you little bitch? Am I supposed to be scared now, you snot-nosed, yellowbellied dog-fucker?"

Drogan hated that kid.

Even now, looking back after more than forty-five years had passed, he wished nothing but the worst pain for that stinking bag of pus from his youth. That was why he could remember his face so well from that day. That was the first time he'd seen that special change come over someone when they finally realized that they were in real trouble.

There was something else that had caught Drogan's attention, even at that young age. It was fear, and he'd sniffed it out so well because he was so intimately familiar with it after feeling it himself for so very long. This time was different, though. This time, Drogan was seeing the fear from the opposite side and he couldn't deny that it was much better from that point of view.

Staring down the barrel of that gun, seeing that cocky asshole's expression turn slowly into the simpering face of a baby girl, Drogan felt as if he'd been reborn. He didn't know much more at the time than that it felt good, and that was enough to make his youthful heart swell.

It only felt better when he heard that asshole start to pretend he wasn't deathly afraid. The teasing stopped and was replaced by clumsy attempts at friendship.

"It was all in fun. We just kid around with each other.
You know that."

Those words still echoed in Drogan's mind, and they
still seemed just as hollow as when he'd heard them the
first time. Although Drogan didn't put one bit of faith in
those words, he listened to every last one. He knew he
would remember them forever, because his finger was already tightening around the stolen gun's trigger.

As that pistol started to shake in Drogan's hand, everyone nearby knew he was going to fire it. That was when
those clumsy words from that prick's mouth shifted into
a frantic stream of begging, which was soon laced with
tears that started flowing down the other kid's face.

Drogan listened to those words also. His jaw clenched
tightly shut and he felt a coldness form in the pit of his
stomach. It felt as though the trigger had rusted in place
because he had a hell of a time pulling it. But his finger
had more than just his little muscles behind it. In that one
skinny finger, there was a lifetime of anger, frustration,
and worst of all, rage.

All of that made him strong enough to do what he
needed to do. He knew that even though he still couldn't
get that trigger to budge more than a fraction of a centi-
meter.

The kid in front of him was crying openly by this
point. The scent of urine filled the air as a dark stain
formed in that asshole's britches. But Drogan didn't smile
at that. Instead, he steeled his gaze and watched like a
judge passing sentence.

And in that one fraction of a moment, Drogan's finger
pulled through the rust that had kept that trigger in place
and he dropped the hammer upon the live round in that
cylinder.

The gun bucked like a wild bronco in his little hand,
but Drogan was holding on with everything he had. That
gun wasn't about to get away from him. Instead, it became

a part of him as it spat out its plume of smoky flame and punched a messy hole right through the middle of that son of a bitch's face.

That punk's brains spewed into the air, and every other kid that had gathered around to witness the fight bolted for home. Drogan stood there with his gun in hand, pulling the smell of burnt gunpowder into his nose. His hands were no longer trembling and he was no longer afraid.

He merely sat down right where he was and set that gun in his lap. The iron was still warm, like a monster who'd come from a storybook to smite his enemy. Drogan looked around and saw that, even though they were keeping their distance from him, the rest of the kids were looking at him with fear and respect.

Drogan stared them down one by one until he finally got up and took his gun home. It was a day that made him into the man who now sat quietly at his table in the back of The Copperhead Saloon. When he looked around at the drunks and gunmen around him, he saw traces of fear and respect.

This time, however, he was only able to stare down about half of them.

ELEVEN

The next morning, Clint woke up feeling rested and happy to be right where he was. Of course, seeing as he was right next to a buxom, naked blonde, it wasn't too difficult to justify feeling that way. His good spirits lasted right up until he took in a deep breath, collected his thoughts, and started to recall what had happened the night before.

Something still didn't sit right with him about Two-Cent Drogan. Something in the back of his mind told him that he wasn't through dealing with the older man, despite the fact that he'd made his position plenty clear back in The Copperhead. But rather than drag that through the dirt some more, Clint pulled his clothes on and stepped out onto his balcony.

When he turned around again, he saw Amanda stretching her arms and making her way slowly over to her dress, which lay in a crumpled heap on the floor. She knew he was watching her, so she took her time dressing and straightening the strands of hair that fell down over her face.

"You trying to torture me or just pull me back into bed with you?" Clint asked.

She smirked and tried to look innocent for a moment,

but even she couldn't keep up that charade for too long. "Maybe a little bit of one and a lot more of the other. By the looks of things, I won't have any luck keeping you here for too long, though."

"Why do you say that?"

"Because the sun's barely up and you're already halfway out the door. Besides, I know you're still fretting about that scrap you had last night."

"And here I thought I had a halfway decent poker face."

"You do, but I know you, Clint Adams. I know you don't like it when things are wrapped up nice and neat. I also know you well enough to know what would make you feel better."

"Any more of that and I may not be able to walk straight," he replied with a laugh.

"I wasn't talking about that! I meant breakfast. How about we go fetch us some steak and eggs?"

At the mere mention of a hearty breakfast, Clint's stomach began to churn greedily inside him. Just then, it felt as though he hadn't had a good meal for at least a week. "I've got to hand it to you. When you say you know a man, you sure aren't fooling. Lead the way."

She made herself presentable as quickly as possible, and took him by the hand from the room and out of the hotel. Outside, the town was bathed in the warm light of dawn and filled with a crisp breeze that held the burgeoning promise of winter. All of those things combined to make Clint feel better about the day, and a whole lot hungrier as well.

Amanda made small talk to a few familiar faces, introducing Clint along the way. For the most part, the town of Plattsmith seemed to be going about its day as if the previous night had been nothing special. Clint had been to plenty of towns where shootings and bar fights were business as usual, but there was usually a bit more tension in the air once the smoke had settled.

Then again, a lot of that tension came from Clint actually taking part in those fights and feeling the aftermath firsthand. This time, he'd dodged the bullet with his name on it, and wasn't even involved with the cleanup.

As if reading his mind yet again, Amanda looked over to Clint and asked, "Do you think that friend of yours is still in town? He might even be in jail, I suppose."

"First of all, Drogan isn't exactly a friend of mine. As for the law, you would probably know about that more than me. Does this town have a lawman that gets involved in bar fights? I've been to more than a few that figure saloon shootings are a kind of way for nature to take its course and clean up their streets without them having to lift a finger."

"Sheriff Carlyle is a good enough sort," was all Amanda really had to say about that.

They were walking up to the restaurant that Amanda had chosen for them and already, Clint could pick out the smell of fresh biscuits and coffee in the air. With those scents in his nose, his priorities were arranged in a much simpler matter without him having to think twice about it.

"You know what?" he said. "Whatever your sheriff does, it's really not my concern. He's the one in charge of this town, not me. So let's just let that sleeping dog lie and let's get us some breakfast."

He got no argument from Amanda, and both of them went inside to help themselves to a heaping plate of eggs, biscuits, and gravy as well as a thick cut of steak. The eggs were a bit runny and the steak had more than its share of gristle, but the coffee was strong and his stomach was quickly filled.

Clint enjoyed only letting himself be concerned with the immediate needs like food and drink. It was a nice change for him to sit back and savor his meal rather than try to fuss with any life-or-death situations. Before they were through with the meal, both he and Amanda were smiling and joking back and forth. They even went for a stroll with no real destination in mind just to walk off their meals.

Plattsmith was located in a scenic area that was thick with trees, all of which were in various stages of the season. Plenty of branches were bare, and the ones still sporting leaves displayed colors ranging from light yellow to deep, rich red. Clint and Amanda's walk took them to the edge of town so they could take in the sights while simply enjoying each other's company.

Neither of them said much once they'd gone past the town's limits. They didn't have to. And even though the silence felt soothing to Clint's ears, it also gave his mind another chance to back up and go over the things that had been bothering him before.

He thought back to Drogan and all he knew of the gunfighter's reputation. He thought about where that man could be at that moment, and wondered if he still had that smoldering flame behind his eyes that had been there in The Copperhead the previous night.

It was at that moment, as if answering the turmoil that was whipping itself up inside Clint's mind, that a single gunshot echoed in the distance. Clint's muscles tensed and he let out a sigh.

"Go on, Clint," Amanda said before he could say a word to her. "Just be careful."

TWELVE

Hours before Clint had had his breakfast, before the sun had even peeked over the horizon, Luke Drogan was still sitting at his table in the back of The Copperhead Saloon. Like a permanent fixture on top of the warped wooden surface, his glass of whiskey was still there. The only thing that was different was the mostly empty bottle that was now standing beside it.

The bartender had brought over the bottle after getting tired of running back and forth to fill Drogan's glass. Normally, he would have told a customer to get his own damn drinks as soon as he became a nuisance. The Copperhead was, after all, known more for its cheap liquor than its sterling customer relations.

The bartender had been keeping a watchful eye on Drogan ever since he'd gunned down one of his regular customers in cold blood. Once the ruckus with that had died down, the drinkers had gone back to their drinking and the gamblers had gone back to their gambling.

But after Clint had left, Drogan hadn't just gone back to his drinking. He'd gone back to his table and dropped down into his chair as if his legs had given out. He'd started drinking more than ever while staring into space as though he was glaring into the eyes of some unseen enemy. And whenever he did speak to someone else, Drogan had more venom in his words than a rattlesnake.

In fact, the barkeep didn't just suspect there might be more blood spilled in his saloon that night; he fully expected it. Rather than provoke Drogan, the barkeep just gave him what he asked for without any fuss. All the while, he'd been hoping the killer would just tip back one more shot of whiskey than he needed and then fall asleep right there at his table.

Unfortunately, Drogan put away the liquor as if he was pounding back shots of water. His eyes didn't lose their focus, but only got meaner. His speech didn't slur, but only became more hateful. It had gone on like that all night long, until finally a ray of hope came through the saloon's front door.

"Hey there," the barkeep said to the new arrival. "I was beginning to think you were never going to make it over here."

The man who walked into the salon was average height and had a slightly bulky build. A man in his late forties, he stared out at the world through eyes that had obviously seen their share. His face was covered with skin so weathered, it made his flesh resemble tree bark, and his hair shot out of his scalp in long, thick tufts beneath a Stetson hat.

"What're you grinning about?" the other man asked as he stepped up to the bar.

"Nothin', Sheriff Carlyle. Hell, I don't have much to grin about after the night I had."

The lawman thought for a moment and then started to nod. "Oh, yeah. There was some trouble here last night, wasn't there?"

Pounding a glass onto the bar, the bartender looked as though he was set to burst. "You know damn well there was trouble here. The question is, where the hell were you?"

"You need me to come down here every time there's a scuffle? If you don't like the fighting in your place, then you should cater to a more respectable crowd. Or serve better beer. That swill you pour is bad enough to make anyone mad enough to kill."

"A man was—" Stopping himself in midstream, the barkeep took a quick look over his shoulder. When he saw Drogan sitting back there, he leaned in closer to the sheriff, lowered his voice, and continued. "A man was shot dead right in front of my place and you act like I'm bitching 'cause my floors are dirty."

"Someone came by to clean up the body and such, didn't they?"

"Yes. They got here faster than you or that lazy farmer you call a deputy."

The sheriff's only response was an icy stare that darted from his empty glass and back up toward the bartender's face. Finally, the barkeep got the message and filled the lawman's glass halfway with the lawman's usual drink.

Sheriff Carlyle took a healthy pull from his glass and set it down. "All right, all right. I take it you saw what happened?"

"Yes, sir. I saw it all. So did everyone in here last night."

"Go on and tell me about it."

The barkeep filled Carlyle in on the fight between Drogan and the young man who'd been quickly turned into a corpse. The story was short and sweet and when it was over, Carlyle was already finished with his drink. To say the expression on the lawman's face was aggravated would have been an understatement.

"So it was a bar fight?" Carlyle asked blandly.

"Well . . . more or less . . . yeah."

"I told you after the third man was gunned down in

this shit-hole of yours that if you were going to serve the scum that rides through here, you could handle the fights yourself. Don't you remember me telling you that?"

"Yeah, but—"

"But nothing. I've got enough to do around here and only half a man to help me do it. I should fine you for wasting my time with this bullshit."

The bartender was getting more nervous the louder Sheriff Carlyle's voice became. Beads of sweat even formed upon his brow as he kept gesturing for the sheriff to quiet down. Of course, the barkeep's insistent gesturing had the exact opposite effect upon the sheriff.

The lawman stopped what he was saying and told the barkeep, "You keep waving at me like that and I'll spill some more blood on this floor."

"I just don't want any more trouble in here, Sheriff. Not the kind of trouble that's in here right now."

"What're you talking about?"

"Right there," he said, pointing toward Drogan. "That's the man that killed—"

"Fine, fine. I'll have a look." With that, Sheriff Carlyle put his drink down and started walking over toward the back table.

THIRTEEN

The fog of alcohol was thick in Drogan's skull. It was so thick that it even clouded the first rays of dawn that were fighting their way toward the back of The Copperhead Saloon. Despite his best effort to dull his senses and his own mind, he was unable to soak enough whiskey into his brain to do the trick. He'd been a drinker his whole life. The simple truth was that it helped to be drunk when sending other people to their graves.

Over the years, his body had just gotten accustomed to the flow of liquor. After downing one and a half bottles all by himself, Drogan still wasn't far enough gone to keep from hearing nearly every word that passed between the barkeep and Sheriff Carlyle.

Drogan would have preferred not to hear the things the sheriff had said. That way, he wouldn't have felt his blood start to boil over with anger. If it was good for anything, the whiskey in his system served to ignite that anger into a burning rage just as easily as if Drogan himself had dropped a lit match into the bottle.

As he watched the sheriff walk toward him, Drogan could hear the voices of his father and that loudmouthed prick kid who'd been Two-Cent's first kill. He heard those voices every time he got himself drunk and angry, but that didn't make his blood boil any cooler.

Sheriff Carlyle had a look on his face as though he was smelling dog shit as he made his way to Drogan's table. He stepped right up to the chair where Clint had sat the night before and kicked the table leg with his left toe.

"All right," Carlyle said. "This ain't a hotel. Sleep it off somewhere else."

"Do I look like I'm sleeping?" Drogan asked.

"No. You look like a man that shot someone dead last night. You're damn lucky you're not in a jail cell right now. So get yourself up and out of here before I take your gun from you and lock your stinking ass away."

Drogan pushed away from the table and picked up his bottle of whiskey. "Care for a drink?"

"I'd just as soon spit a mouthful of whiskey at you than drink it with you. Now get the fuck out of here."

That was the one chance Drogan was willing to give for the sheriff to redeem himself. Having failed the test miserably, the lawman scowled like just another one of the loudmouthed, hotheaded, ignorant pieces of shit polluting Drogan's world.

"Actually, Sheriff," Drogan said, holding the bottle up in one hand, "I insist." With that, Drogan swung the bottle in a short arc toward the sheriff's head. He did this without flinching or so much as a blink that might tip his hand that he was about to move.

Even if Carlyle hadn't had a stiff shot of whiskey only moments ago, it was doubtful that he would have seen anything coming. He did manage to get out a surprised cry before trying to duck. All of this was too late, however, and the bottle smashed into the side of his head.

Despite Drogan's strength and quick, snapping swing, the bottle didn't break. Instead, it bounced off the lawman's skull with a dull thump. The sheriff's eyes glazed over, and he made a sloppy reach for his gun as Drogan came around with another swing.

This time, having cocked his arm all the way back and swinging forward with his entire body leaning into it, Drogan was able to shatter the bottle against Carlyle's head. The gunfighter was surprised when the sheriff somehow remained on his feet. Not only that, but Carlyle was still reaching for his holstered revolver.

Drogan may have been surprised by the sheriff's tenacity, but he wasn't about to let himself catch a bullet because of it. Still holding the jagged piece of the bottle in his right hand, Drogan made a crossover reach for his copper-plated .44. He cleared leather and flipped the gun so he was holding it correctly in what should have been a fatal amount of time.

If Carlyle had been able to see straight, he would have easily gunned Drogan down where he stood. As it was, however, the sheriff was hardly able to keep from dropping his weapon while staggering back to bump against the next table. He still managed to draw his weapon and pull his trigger, sending a noisy shot into the floor several feet short of where Drogan was standing.

The copper-handled pistol spit a gout of fire toward the lawman, digging a chunk from Carlyle's hip. Drogan stood and readied himself to pull his trigger a second time. The only thing staying his hand for the moment was that he was too busy watching Carlyle's wounded leg buckle and the rest of his body drop toward the floor.

Somehow, the sheriff was able to catch himself before falling over completely. The flow of adrenaline through his body and the sound of gunfire was better than a splash of cold water in sobering him up. Even so, he was still wounded in two places, which made him both groggy and off balance.

Not a good combination when lead was headed his way.

Drogan knew better than to wait around for the sheriff's aim to improve, and was already moving before Carlyle could regain his balance. He walked past the sheriff. Using his free hand, Drogan pushed the lawman over as if he was knocking an empty barrel onto its side. He had his gun ready to take another shot, but that wasn't necessary since Carlyle hit the floor on his wounded hip.

The sheriff was able to stifle a pained scream, which forced a sound out of him much like a man buried under a few feet of dirt. After sucking in a breath, however, he was able to get out a few words that rolled through the saloon and even made it out through the batwing doors.

"Jack," Carlyle shouted. "Kill this son of a bitch!"

FOURTEEN

Even though he'd never met Jack personally, Drogan was fairly sure the sheriff was shouting to the burly, younger man waiting outside wearing the deputy's badge. Drogan had made it out of the saloon and nearly past the deputy when the sheriff's scratchy voice rolled outside.

The deputy responded instantly by drawing his gun and looking for a target. Even though Drogan was in plain sight, Jack wasn't sure if he really should just shoot the first man to come walking out of The Copperhead. His dilemma was cut short when he saw Drogan lifting his arm and aiming his gun directly at him.

The men on either side of that copper-plated weapon could tell the hand holding it was more than a little shaky. Drogan still had speed on his side, however, and he got a shot off a full second before Jack the deputy could pull his trigger.

Drogan's gun fired off a round that roared through the air and echoed up and down the street. The voice of the .44 rumbled like thunder as the man who'd fired it took a few calm steps backward and into the street.

The deputy's body had jerked back in response to the shot, and he crumpled inward while shuffling sideways

toward whatever cover he could find. Even though the
post in front of the saloon wasn't even wide enough to
cover half his body, Jack straightened against it and re-
gained some of his confidence.

From there, the deputy leaned around the post and took
aim with his gun. Another shot rang through the air,
quickly followed by the hiss of incoming lead and the
crunch of splintering wood. Once again, the deputy pulled
away and ducked behind the post as if the narrow piece
of lumber could actually protect him.

The next shot from Drogan's gun would have no doubt
done some serious damage. The only saving grace for the
deputy was that Drogan didn't fire again. Instead, the gunfighter turned his back on the lawman and quickly walked
down the street.

Drogan didn't feel the need to run. His blood was still
coursing through him like a hot current, and his nerves
tingled with the anticipation of the next shot, which just
might drive a round into his body. But even with all of
that, he kept his walk swift without breaking into a run
or even a jog. Instead, he just walked to the nearest cross-
road and turned the corner.

"Stop where you are!" Jack shouted. "Stop or I'll
shoot!"

But the deputy was still holding right where he was
behind his chipped, narrow post. Every so often, his eyes
would dart toward the splintered spot where the last bullet
had gone, and that sight alone would keep the rest of him
from budging.

Jack nearly jumped straight into the air when the saloon's doors flapped open and Sheriff Carlyle came storm-
ing out. The bigger man had one hand clamped to the
bleeding wound on his hip, and was trying to look out
through the one eye that wasn't swollen shut. Because of
those things, the only thing he could see clearly was the
deputy right in front of him.

"What the hell happened out here?" Carlyle bellowed. "Where'd that bastard get to? He'd better be wounded, Jack, or I swear to God I'll wound *you*."

Even though Drogan wasn't even in sight any longer, Jack was still having a hard time getting his back to give up the comfort of that post. "I didn't have time, Sheriff. It all happened so fast, I just—"

"Save it." The sheriff meant to tear into Jack some more, but he held his tongue. After all, Drogan had gotten away from him as well, so he couldn't exactly hold a deputy to a higher standard. "Do you at least know which way he went?"

Jack peeled himself away from the post and nodded in the direction that Drogan had walked. "There's got to be more of them, Sheriff," Jack said in his own defense. "He's probably just waiting for us to come after him so he can take another shot at us."

"Then you'd best keep your eyes open, because I'm not about to let him just up and walk away from the both of us! Come on."

Sheriff Carlyle walked with a surprising amount of strength for a man in his condition. It was sheer stubbornness that kept his head up and his steps relatively steady. He was still wounded, however, and when he reached the top step leading from the boardwalk onto the street, he nearly fell face-first into the dirt.

Jack was able to reach out and grab the sheriff's elbow before he tripped, and knew enough not to hold on for very long since Carlyle quickly pulled his arm back.

Both lawmen had their guns drawn and were ready to fire at the first sign of movement that caught their eye. Luckily for the general population, anyone who'd been in Plattsmith for more than a few days knew just to steer clear of The Copperhead if and when any shots were fired. The street was clear as Carlyle and his deputy turned the corner, although several people watched from a safe distance.

"Where'd he go?" Carlyle asked.

Jack was walking to the left and slightly behind Sheriff Carlyle. At first, the deputy replied with a shrug and shake of his head. Knowing Carlyle couldn't see him, he quickly added, "I can't rightly say, Sheriff. I saw him go this direction."

"Go back to The Copperhead and find out where he's staying. If anyone in town knows, that barkeep's the one. If he's staying in one of those stink-hole rooms upstairs in that place, get inside and see what you can see."

"What about you?" Jack asked. "You sure you can do this on yer own seeing as how you're—"

"Just shut the hell up and do what you were told. If he's not renting a room in that saloon, come get me."

Knowing better than to argue with Carlyle when he was in a mood like this one, Jack turned and jogged back to the saloon.

Carlyle walked about three more steps before he spotted the shape of an armed man headed straight for him. There was still a bloody haze blurring his vision, but Carlyle could see enough to tighten his grip around his own pistol and start picking out his target.

He wasn't about to get caught flat-footed again, even if it meant gunning that son of a bitch down without so much as a how-do-you-do.

FIFTEEN

Clint heard the second gunshot when he was running down First Avenue. He'd figured that the initial shot had come from the vicinity of The Copperhead, and hearing that second shot only confirmed that in his mind. That sound also made him quicken his pace, until he damn near lost his footing while coming around the next corner.

Several people were on either side of the street, going about their normal morning routines. Clint sped around, past, and even between them on his way to the saloon, hoping he wasn't too late to prevent yet another fatality. That sneaking suspicion was nagging at him once more. It told him that those shots didn't mark just another violent day in a bad saloon.

The sight of Drogan's angry, violent eyes still hung in Clint's mind. He'd known that Two-Cent wasn't finished after being denied the fight he truly wanted. If giving him that fight was the fastest way to end Drogan's shooting spree, then Clint figured he might have to do just that.

Clint sped around the corner like a bull with its tail on fire, and immediately spotted the other man headed straight toward him. Reacting on instinct after spotting the gun in the other man's hand, Clint drew his modified Colt and held it at the ready.

A few more quick steps brought him close enough to make out the other man's face. It wasn't the face he'd been expecting, which caused him to lower the Colt. Despite that move on his part, Clint could tell that the other man wasn't reacting with the same courtesy.

The man in front of him was moving with slow, deliberate movements that seemed stiff and even mechanical. Even so, there was a good amount of speed in his arm as the other man lifted his gun and took aim.

Clint's body reacted without him having to think about it. All he needed to see was that the other man was preparing to fire, and Clint was already dodging to one side. The Colt was ready to fire as well, but Clint refrained from pulling the trigger.

That restraint became a downright struggle when the man in front of him took a shot and sent a bullet through the air. Clint could hear the hiss of speeding lead well enough to tell that the shot hadn't even come close to hitting him. When he came to a stop at the side of the street, Clint threw up both hands and shouted loud enough to be heard over the echo of gunfire.

"Whoever you are, don't shoot!"

The other man stopped and held his gun up to take more careful aim.

Now that he was stopped and had a chance to take a better look at the other man, Clint was able to pick out the glint of steel pinned to the figure's chest. "I heard the shots, Sheriff," Clint said. "I just came by to help."

Carlyle stopped just short of firing again, and took a moment to wipe away some of the blood that had dripped into his eye. The other eye was swollen shut, making it impossible for him to see much more than shapes and blurs of motion. Now that he'd taken a moment to survey his surroundings, the lawman lowered his pistol.

"Step closer," Carlyle ordered. "And lower that gun!"

Clint did as he was told, and holstered the Colt to prevent any more confusion.

The sheriff relaxed, but kept his own weapon drawn. After taking a few more steps himself, he squinted his one good eye to get a better look at the person standing in front of him. Once he saw that he had indeed taken a shot at the wrong man, Carlyle tried to keep control of the situation. "There's an armed man who just went by here. Did you see him?"

"No. I heard the shots and was just coming to see if I could lend a hand."

"Well, you can't, so just get off the street and keep out of my way."

Clint wasn't about to trade more angry words with the lawman, so he stepped aside and let Carlyle pass. With Drogan's face in his mind as fresh as if he'd just finished talking to him, Clint began his own search of the area. With the sheriff running so fast, his target had to be nearby. Clint kept that in mind and quickly began checking the area. If the armed man the sheriff was looking for wasn't Drogan, then it was probably just another bit of unrelated business.

There were plenty of armed men in Plattsmith.

There were plenty of shootings in the vicinity of The Copperhead Saloon.

But something in the back of Clint's mind told him that Drogan's face was the one the sheriff was looking for as well. Anything else would have made Clint's life too easy.

SIXTEEN

After roughly half an hour of searching the area as well as the adjacent streets, Clint figured Drogan had given everyone the slip. There was also the possibility that Drogan wasn't the armed man in question, so Clint headed back to The Copperhead to clear that up.

It didn't take much of a detective for Clint to realize that his first instinct had indeed been correct. Not only was Drogan missing from his table, but his name was being tossed around like a hot potato by everyone inside the saloon. No more than a few minutes after he'd arrived, Clint saw another familiar figure step through the batwing doors.

Actually, limping through the doors would have been a more accurate description.

Sheriff Carlyle made his way into the saloon and headed straight for the bar as if he was just another thirsty customer. A whiskey was set in front of him without anything said to the barkeep, and was drained with one gulp. The lawman set it down roughly and locked eyes with the barkeep.

"Was my deputy even in here?" Carlyle asked.

The barkeep nodded quickly and said, "Yeah. He's still here. Upstairs in Mr. Drogan's room."

"So you know who that was that did all that shooting?"

"Yeah. Two-Cent Drogan."

"And you didn't think to tell me that much before?"

"You didn't give me much of a chance to say anything but where he was."

"Which room was he in?"

"Number four." Grabbing reflexively for a key underneath the bar, the barkeep came up short and waved toward a narrow door at the other end of the bar. "Your deputy has the key. He's still up there."

Carlyle didn't say another word as he limped along the length of the bar. When he got next to where Clint was standing, he paused and turned to look him in the eye. "I thought I told you to get clear of this."

The stench of alcohol burned from Carlyle's mouth so strongly that Clint could feel the burn of whiskey in his own throat. That, combined with what he'd seen of Carlyle's behavior, didn't do much to bolster his opinion of the lawman. "You told me to get off the street, Sheriff. I did."

"Smart-ass, huh? What's your name?"

"Clint Adams."

"Oh, is it now? I heard you were in town. You know, it's gunmen like you that give good towns like this one a bad name."

"I'm the least of this town's problems, Sheriff. Besides, I was having a perfectly good time on my own when all this shooting started. I'd be happy to lend a hand, though, if you—"

Carlyle stopped him with a quickly raised hand. "Spare me the offer, Adams. I'm sure the town's coffers don't have enough to cover your price. Besides, it'll be a cold day in hell before I take help from one'a the gunmen that I'd love to see run out of here altogether."

Clint might have been offended by those comments if it had come from the mouth of someone not so drunk or from a man he halfway respected. As it was, Clint merely shrugged, stepped aside, and swept his arm toward the door graciously. "Then, by all means, Sheriff, you do whatever you see fit."

Carlyle kept his eyes focused on Clint. The one was still swollen shut, but with some effort on his part, he could force it open into a narrow squint. His face was already twisted into a scowl with the swelling on one side, and he let out a grunting breath as he got himself moving once again.

Watching the sheriff make his way painfully through the narrow door and then up a flight of narrow stairs, Clint wondered if the lawman truly expected to get anything done. More than likely, he was just going through the motions of doing his job to kill time until his next drink.

Clint didn't bother trying to get a look at Drogan's room for himself. A seasoned killer like Two-Cent was always ready to get up and go. In fact, Clint had a good guess as to what the two men looking around up there would find. Probably nothing more than a few bits of clothing and maybe a razor. One thing was for damn sure: Two-Cent Drogan wouldn't be anywhere near that room and he wouldn't have left anything telling the law where he might go.

Drogan himself probably didn't even know where he might go until he was halfway there.

Satisfied that he'd found all there was to find in The Copperhead, Clint turned his back on the table that he'd shared with Drogan and left. From there, he went straight back to his hotel. Along the way, he passed the little bakery that always smelled of fresh bread, and couldn't help but glance in through the large front window.

Amanda was standing in there much as she'd been when Clint had first come into town. And just like that reunion only a few short days ago, she spotted him and came running out to catch him before he could get any further down the boardwalk.

"Where you headed, Clint?" she asked, falling into step beside him.

"I'm going back to my room so I can collect my things and head out of town."

"What? Why? I thought you could stay for a while."

"Things have changed, Amanda. I'll come back as soon as I can, though, all right?"

She picked up her speed just enough to get in front of him and plant her feet. "Hold it. So you're just leaving?"

Even though he'd seen her jumping in front of him, Clint still nearly walked right into her. He stopped short, thanks in part to her outstretched hands. "Let's just say I've gotten a good look at the law in this town and know that if I don't go after Drogan, no one else will."

"If he's gone, then why does anyone have to go after him?"

"Because I got a good look at his eyes. There's something wrong in that head of his. He'll keep coming after me and will kill others along the way. If I track him down myself, I'll save him the trouble of gunning men down to get my attention again."

"And you're sure this isn't a matter for the sheriff to handle?"

Clint started to laugh, but without a bit of humor in his tone. "I've seen enough of your sheriff to see why so many folks around here don't bat an eye when they hear shooting in their streets. In fact, I'm surprised there isn't more lawlessness just because that sheriff is more interested in using his badge to get himself free drinks."

She reached out and ran her hands over Clint's shoulders before reaching up to hold his face in a gentle grasp. "I've heard about this man Drogan too. Folks say he's dead inside already and will kill a man for no reason at all."

"Part of that may be true," Clint replied, placing his hands over hers. "But he's got a reason for killing just like he's got a reason for coming after me. I just need to find out what it is."

Amanda studied his face for another second or two before planting a kiss on his lips. The kiss was gentle at first, but gained momentum and quickly became more heated than even she'd expected. "I've seen that look in your eyes before, but that doesn't mean I have to like it. I'm not going to tell you to be careful again, so just re-member to come see me when this is straightened out. All right?"

Nodding, Clint said, "You've got yourself a deal."

As Clint left Amanda standing in front of the bakery, he could tell that she still didn't fully understand why he had to track down a killer who'd already left town on his own. The truth of the matter was that his decision had nothing to do with good sense.

It was a matter of instinct.

Where Luke Drogan's instinct was to kill, Clint's was to stop him.

Plain and simple.

SEVENTEEN

Drogan had left town carrying nothing but what was either in his pockets or strapped around his waist. His horse was in a rented stall on the edge of town, and after he'd gotten the animal saddled, Drogan paid the liveryman and was on his way.

The grizzled fellow running the stable was about Drogan's age. When Two-Cent had handed over an extra two dollars and asked only a single favor in return, he'd agreed readily enough. Actually, the liveryman would have done that favor for free, but Drogan wasn't about to take advantage of a man just because he could.

It was a funny thing, making that one little decision. Drogan could just as easily have saved his money and gotten that liveryman to cooperate out of fear for his life. A snarled threat and a quick draw of his pistol would have done the trick nicely, but Drogan thought that would have been wrong.

The irony of that didn't escape the killer, and gave him something to ponder on his ride away from Plattsmith. As he rode, he didn't touch his heels to his horse's sides or even give the reins much more than the occasional snap.

He wasn't in too big of a hurry to leave the town, after all.

He knew the sheriff was too stupid to know where he'd gone until it was too late, and too lazy to come after him even when he did. That deputy was too scared to look in Drogan's direction after their little run-in.

That only left one other for Drogan to worry about. Clint Adams was just the sort with the skill and gumption to track him down after everything Drogan had done. The only question in Two-Cent's mind was if Adams would decide to come after him.

If he did, that was just fine with Drogan.

If Adams decided to move along, then that just gave Drogan some more time to finish his own business before his next meeting with The Gunsmith. There was still plenty on Drogan's plate. The task he'd given to himself wasn't small by any stretch of the imagination, but it was the most important thing in his life.

No, that wasn't quite right.

It was his whole life.

It was the one thing that kept Drogan moving even though his tired old body wanted nothing more than to keep still. It also kept the whiskey flowing down his throat to keep him numb until that important task was done.

He was close now. Closer than he'd ever been to completing this task that had occupied his mind to some degree or another for the better part of his life. Well, it had hung over him ever since he'd gotten the name of Two-Cent.

Drogan looked back on that as a kind of rebirth. It was the day when that scared, helpless little runt that he'd been was killed and buried deep. Ever since then, there had been one driving force inside of him that had kept him riding from town to town and not leaving until the taste of gunpowder was thick in his throat.

At the start of his new life, even Drogan himself hadn't

known what this thing was that had kept him going. He'd just taken it for granted that he was a man of the gun. A killer. A gunfighter. Whatever the word someone chose to describe his murderous ways, Drogan would never dispute it.

On the contrary, he'd welcomed those names because every last one of them was better than the names he'd had for himself before.

Coward.

Weakling.

Victim.

Being called a cold-blooded killer was a hell of a lot better than being called those things. Even now, in his twilight years, Drogan knew that to be true. The only thing left for him to do was to live up to his adopted title right up to the end.

And that end was coming.

It might even come to him in Mehlville Crossing. That was the name posted on the sign outside the small town that Drogan rode into after his short ride. The place wasn't too far from Plattsmith, but was small enough that it was easy to overlook even by members of that nearby community. It was also far enough away that a lawman as lazy as Sheriff Carlyle would probably consider it too far from his office to bother tracking him down there.

Drogan gazed around at the shabby buildings and took a careful look behind him. There was nobody paying him too much mind from either side of the street, and there wasn't anyone behind him. He knew that wouldn't last long, however.

In fact, he'd see to it that it didn't.

EIGHTEEN

Clint had gotten enough information from the liveryman to give him a start on tracking Drogan. The other man hadn't known exactly where Two-Cent was heading, but he did watch long enough to see which direction he'd ridden out of town. It wasn't much to go by, but Clint used that as a starting point and headed off from there.

The weather was cooperating enough for him to have no trouble spotting fresh tracks leading away from the stable. Drogan had probably chosen the place with a quick getaway in mind, but its remoteness worked to Clint's advantage as well. There weren't many tracks at all leading from the place, and only one set heading out of town in the proper direction.

With no other leads to follow, Clint set his sights on those tracks and flicked Eclipse's reins. The Darley Arabian wanted to stretch his legs a bit more, but didn't try to go against his rider's lead. Clint kept his pace slow until he hit a well-worn trail outside of town, and then he let Eclipse cut loose a bit more.

Clint would stop every so often to make sure he still had the tracks in his sight. They never once varied from where he thought they'd be simply because Clint had a pretty good idea of where Drogan would be headed anyway.

Someone like Drogan wasn't exactly the camping type. Surely, he would make camp when necessary, and even live in the wilds for extended amounts of time when he was on the run, but no longer than what was needed. Drogan was a gunfighter, first and foremost. Gunfighters were, by nature, town and city folk.

After all, there wasn't much to keep someone occupied on the trail who was looking for street fights and the glory of combat. Clint had been around plenty of those types to know that much for sure. Most fighting men would even pass through a town no matter how tired they were if there wasn't at least one saloon.

Having been through the area enough to know it fairly well, Clint thought about where someone like Drogan would head once he was no longer welcome in Plattsmith. The closest place that would suit a man like that was a little settlement named Mehlville Crossing.

The last time Clint had gone there, it wasn't much more than a large camp set up to give railroad workers a place to sleep. It was rough, mostly lawless, and had more saloons than stores. In short, it had been the perfect place for a gunfighter to find some action, and Clint doubted that it had changed too much.

When he arrived, it was after a full day's ride and the sun was already out of the sky. Although he'd taken his time in getting there, every step of the way had been used trying to keep an eye on tracks that disappeared like smoke in the fading daylight. He might have been able to get there in half the time if he hadn't been following that specific set of tracks, but he hadn't wanted to let them out of his sight just in case Drogan had tried to pull something unexpected.

In a way, the fact that those tracks hadn't taken one unexpected turn annoyed Clint by the end of the day. That was because he would have been better off just following the trail and letting Eclipse run full out the way he'd wanted to the entire time. Clint's sour attitude was also due to the fact that he'd climbed on and off the stallion enough times to put a knot in his back the size of Texas.

By the time he finally arrived in Mehlville Crossing, Clint was about ready to forget about the tracks that had led him there just so he could rest his weary eyes and aching bones. Drogan could have been sitting alongside the road at any point as Clint rode into town and would have gone unnoticed. All Clint was looking for by that time was a hotel, and when he found one, he tied Eclipse up in front of it and walked inside.

For a moment, Clint thought he'd wandered into the wrong building by mistake. He found himself in what appeared to be a modest home with nobody even inside it. Just as he was going to turn around and walk back outside, he was greeted by a woman in her early fifties who came rushing in from the next room.

"Sorry about that," she said with a flustered smile. "I was just cleaning up the dinner dishes. Are you here to rent a room?"

"Yes, I am," Clint said, still looking around for any outward sign that he was standing in a hotel. "Are there any available?"

The woman rushed right past him and disappeared through a narrow little door that Clint hadn't even seen until she'd opened it. Her steps could be heard shuffling behind the wall, and then she reappeared in what had at first looked like a darkened window looking in on a storage space. The woman lit a lantern and hung it on a wall, allowing Clint to see she was actually in a small office.

Her round face was covered with a friendly smile. After she let out a tired breath, she fixed her bright, cheerful eyes on Clint. "All right then. There's one room available, but it doesn't have much of a view. For an extra dollar, though, I'll throw in a free breakfast and a bath." Lowering her voice to a whisper, she winked and said, "You look hungry, so I'll fix you up with some leftovers as well. No charge, of course, since you'll be helping me by giving me less to toss out."

Despite the aching in his back, Clint couldn't help but return the woman's smile. "How could I refuse that? I'll take the room plus the extras. And if those leftovers are as good as they smell, I might just eat a few of the plates while I'm at it."

Looking down, she giggled to herself and scribbled something on a ledger that Clint couldn't see. Her smile was warm as ever as she lifted the book onto the edge of the window and turned it to face him. "Here," she said, handing a pencil out as well. "Just sign on the line I marked and I'll get you your key."

As he signed the ledger, Clint scanned it for any other familiar names. The only other name that was written in vaguely fresh ink was Megan Walsh. The name as well as the handwriting were distinctly feminine, so Clint hoped that there were other rooms to rent in town. If not, then Drogan was getting one hell of a head start.

NINETEEN

Already, Clint was feeling better than when he'd walked in. He was still tired as hell, but he no longer felt like he was going to fall over where he stood. "Is there a place for me to put my horse up for the night nearby?" he asked, putting some stress on that last word.

"Sure is. Right across the street." She handed him a key tied to a faded ribbon and said, "Just let yourself in when you come back and head for the dining room. I'll set a place for you with those leftovers, but you've got to clean up after yourself. Deal?"

"Yes, ma'am," Clint said as though he was talking to a schoolteacher or distant relative. "Thank you."

"No problem. It's good to have nice people like yourself coming to town instead of the dregs that we've been getting lately. And please, Mr. . . . " She paused to turn the register back around so she could read the most recent signature. "Mr. Adams. If you need anything at all, don't hesitate to find me. My name is Anne, so just shout if you can't find me in this old house."

Clint thought about asking Anne about any other new arrivals in town. He figured she would know about those kinds of things even if that new arrival hadn't gotten a

77

room in her own hotel. But he was already starting to feel his energy fade once more, and decided to get Eclipse put up for the night before he lost his ambition to do that as well.

"Thanks, Anne," Clint said after pocketing his key and heading for the door. "I'll be right back to see what I can do about those leftovers."

With that, Clint walked outside again, and found that the darkness had fallen over Mehlville Crossing like a blanket. It was late in the fall, which meant that the sunlight didn't get much time to shine anyhow. Even so, sometimes the nights felt especially cold and barren. It was almost as if the world itself was just as stark and empty as the branches on the trees.

Part of that was due to the lack of any lanterns hanging nearby to illuminate any part of the street. With the sun missing and the sliver of a moon covered by a thick layer of clouds, the only light remaining came as a trickle from a few nearby windows. That didn't do much more than mark the buildings themselves, leaving the rest of the street in inky blackness.

It took a moment, but Clint's eyes finally adjusted to the darkness. Eclipse was waiting right where he'd left him, and the stallion let out a questioning snort while tugging against the reins, which were wrapped around a post.

"Don't worry, boy," Clint said, patting the stallion on the nose. "I didn't forget about you. If I get a warm bed tonight, then so do you."

Once he'd loosened the reins from where they'd been tied, Clint glanced across the street. He quickly spotted the livery that Anne had told him about. He couldn't make out a sign in the darkness, but it was easily twice the size of any other buildings nearby.

Clint led the Darley Arabian across the street and toward the looming shape of the stable. As he got closer,

Clint could see the faint flicker of light moving behind the double set of huge, closed doors. When he was close enough, Clint reached out to knock on those doors, and waited for a response.

The rattle of the doors against their hinges made more noise than Clint's knocking, but there was still no answer. After trying one more time to get someone's attention with no luck, Clint simply put his hand flat against one of the doors and pushed. It swung open with a rusty shriek that passed through the whole door like a shiver.

"Hello?" Clint called out. "Anyone here?"

The faint light he'd spotted outside was a lantern all right, but the movement wasn't because of anyone carrying it from place to place. Instead, the lantern was hanging from a post that formed part of a stall occupied by a fidgeting mule. The mangy animal shifted on its feet and bumped against the post, causing the lantern to swing lazily over a couple bales of hay.

Apart from that one mule, there wasn't anything else that Clint could see that was moving at all. That wouldn't have been too surprising considering that he was in a small town after dark where visitors weren't expected and possibly not even that welcome.

Clint walked deeper into the stable leading Eclipse along with him. His eyes darted back and forth in search of someone who might be working there, or even a notice of what to do if there was a horse that needed a stall for the night.

He found neither.

"Hello?" Clint shouted again, this time a bit louder.

He froze right where he was when he heard sounds deeper within the building. The sounds were something solid shifting against the floor as well as over his head. There was a loft up there that looked about ready to collapse at any second.

The instant he was sure those sounds were footsteps,

Clint's nerves began to twitch beneath his skin. Those steps were too light to belong to anything with four legs, and there were too many of them for it to be just one or two liverymen. The biggest problem, however, was that the light cast by that single lantern wasn't nearly strong enough for him to see who was there and exactly where they were coming from.

Before he let himself get too worked up, Clint said, "I just need a stall for my horse here. If there's no room, I can move along."

There was no reply, but the footsteps had come to a stop.

"I can pay in advance," Clint added as an extra incentive for a real liveryman.

The steps coming from the back of the stable sounded once more, and this time they didn't stop until two figures stepped into the dim light of the building's only source of light. Both of the men were shabbily dressed and wearing tattered jackets over several layers of worn clothes.

They were also both armed, and both had their hands already on the grips of their guns. Their eyes were fixed on Clint as they moved forward like bobcats stalking their prey. Clint could feel more eyes staring daggers into him, and he knew he was being watched from the loft as well.

It was clear he wasn't about to get as warm a reception here as he did in the hotel.

TWENTY

"You can pay in advance, huh?" one of the men said. "Well, I'll only charge you for the next minute or two, because you won't be livin' much longer than that."

Letting Eclipse's reins drop from his hand, Clint squared his shoulders to the pair in front of him and craned his neck to look up at the shadowy loft. Although he couldn't see more than a few dark shapes up there, he craned his neck around slowly to let the others know that he at least knew they were there.

"If you men own this stable," Clint said, "this is one sorry way to run a business."

"That's real funny, stranger. Now let's just see how long you can keep laughing while you're bleedin' out on the floor."

Clint felt each moment tick by in his mind. Judging by the looks of the two in front of him, the minute or two they gave him to live was no joke. The eyes that he could see were like slitted snake's eyes, staring back at him hungrily and expectant of the kill.

"I think you fellas have me confused with someone else," Clint said. "If I walked in on something here, I'll be happy to leave you to it. Like I said, all I need is a stall for my horse."

"You walked into something, all right. But you won't be walkin' out of it, that's for damn sure."

Clint's time was running out. He was as certain of that as if he could actually watch the bottom half of an hourglass filling with sand. "Who are you people?" Clint asked. Since he couldn't get much worse off, he decided to just say what was on his mind. "And if you're so set on picking a fight, what the hell are you doing laying around in a barn?"

"We're the men that own this town and we go where we please. All you need to know is that we been expectin' you." Craning his neck to look up toward the loft, the scruffy man said, "All right, boys. Let's get this done with!"

At that moment, Clint still didn't know who the hell those men were or why they were so angry with him. What he did know was that he wasn't about to get any answers just yet. Three more faces poked out from the shadows over his head, and one more stepped up from the side not too far from where he was standing. Just beneath each of those faces was the glint of drawn iron pointed in his direction.

That one man to his left came as a surprise because Clint didn't know that someone had managed to sneak up that close to him. Rather than be taken aback by that surprise, Clint decided to turn it to his advantage.

His right hand flashed down to draw his modified Colt while his left hand reached out to grab the man who'd just made his presence known. Clint's fingers closed around the Colt's grip an instant before he grabbed the nearby man's shirt. With a simultaneous motion, he brought up the Colt and pulled the other man toward him.

Clint took a moment to make one of the gravest mistakes any man in a fight could ever make. He hesitated before pulling his trigger so he could get a better look at his targets. The only reason he did that was because he could tell instantly that his quick reflexes had put him slightly ahead of all the other men around him. In that time, he was able to size up his opponents and pick out the one among them who was closest to pulling his trigger.

That unlucky soul was one of the men in the loft, and he was just about to take his shot when Clint adjusted his aim and squeezed his own trigger. The modified Colt barked once and sent a round up to the loft. It punched into the other man's forehead and sent him straight back into the shadows. The sound of his body thumping against the bottom of the loft rumbled like thunder over the other men's heads.

Dust rained down onto the first two men who'd greeted Clint as they ducked their heads down and fired off a few panicked rounds. Their fingers clenched around their triggers, throwing off their aim before their hammers even got a chance to drop. The roar of their pistols joined the fire coming from above, turning the inside of the stable into a scene of chaos and confusion.

What animals there were in the stalls started bucking and pounding against the walls. Even Eclipse was getting nervous with all the fire echoing around his head, but he was used to the sound of gunfire enough to keep from bolting altogether.

Now that he'd pulled the closest man to him, Clint saw that the fellow had kept enough of his wits about him to hold onto his gun. More than that, he was bringing that gun around to take a shot point-blank into Clint's stomach.

Clint snapped his Colt straight down so the handle cracked against the other man's wrist. The man let out a sharp yelp as pain stabbed up along his arms and down through his fingers, causing him to drop the pistol before he was able to prevent it. The next thing he felt was a duller pain as the barrel of Clint's Colt was driven straight into his gut just below his rib cage. That impact made him light on his feet as the breath was forced from his lungs and his vision started to blur.

Clint was ready when the man in his grasp started to keel over, and was able to keep him somewhat on his feet. Using that man as a shield, Clint swung his gun hand over the man's shoulder and fired off a round into that troublesome loft. He didn't much like the idea of shooters being able to sneak around up there and take advantage of their valuable higher ground.

The shot he fired hissed through the air and clipped one of the men who had been taking aim at him from above. There was a pained look on his face and a spray of blood, but the crimson mist came from the side, which told Clint that it was probably just a glancing blow. It still stopped that man from firing, and that was just going to have to do for the moment.

Having ducked into one of the nearby stalls, the man that had been doing all the talking before stuck his head out and took a shot at Clint, which whipped inches away from his head. When he opened his mouth, he said the very words that Clint had been hoping not to hear.

"Everyone hold off and when I give the word, you all fire at once!"

Clint winced at the sound of those men getting a real attack organized. When that attack came, living through it would be like trying to stay dry by dodging raindrops. With sheer numbers on their side and a flow in the right direction, they didn't even have to aim.

TWENTY-ONE

"Ready!" the man shouted from the stall.

Clint's mind raced, stretching out every second until it seemed to last ten times as long. Even with the ability to think clearly, that didn't change the fact that there were at least four men remaining and there was that same amount of bullets in the Colt. With all of the men already behind solid cover, that meant Clint would have to be real good and even more than lucky to take down those men.

Unfortunately, he doubted they were going to let him get out of there without putting at least a few bullets in him, and not even a gambler as skilled as himself was that lucky.

Clint could feel the other man preparing to give the order to fire as if he was taking that breath himself. That left him with precious fractions of a second to figure out how to make it out of that stable alive.

Suddenly, his brain fixed on something specific that had caught his attention when he'd first walked into that drafty old building. With no more time to waste, Clint launched himself into motion before hell itself started to rain down upon him. He turned himself while keeping the other man in front of him so he could take quick, careful aim.

So far, the others had done as they were told and the firing had stopped. Clint wasn't about to waste one more moment of that before his own weapon broke the tense, momentary calm. The modified Colt was pointing toward one of the stalls and he pulled his trigger in the final tick of silence before the storm.

"Fi—" was all the man in the stall got to say before Clint's pistol barked and spit its lead toward him.

Although he could have taken out that man with that round, Clint knew that wouldn't keep the rest of them from firing. Instead, he'd fired at a spot just above the other man's head and managed to hit his target perfectly.

The bullet sliced through the lantern's handle like it was butter, sending the lantern straight down onto the hay below. That bullet didn't stop there, however, and kept passing through the post just as Clint had hoped it would. Although the lead was diverted by going through the timber, it flew out the other side at an angle good enough to take a bite out of the mule that had already worked itself into a lather.

As soon as it hit the hay bale, the lantern cracked and spilled its contents, which was immediately set ablaze by the lit wick. Before the flames could grow to much more than a flicker, the mule let out a panicked whinny and lashed out with its powerful hind legs. The impact shook all three walls of the stall and stirred up some confused shouts from the men that had been hiding in there.

Clint smirked to himself and turned his attention back toward the loft. With that angry beast on their backs, the two down below were out of Clint's hair for a little while. He was just in time to send a round up at one of the men looking down on him before that one put Clint down.

The Colt sent its fiery load through the air, which was now filling with smoke. It slapped against flesh and punched a third eye into the skull of the man who'd been taking careful aim at Clint. It was only Clint's lightning quickness that saved his life, and the other man's gun went off only because of a reflexive jerk of the gunman's finger.

At that moment, the man Clint had been holding onto must have caught some breath because he started to kick and thrash in an attempt to get away. Right as he was about to break free, he felt his stomach get knocked up into his throat thanks to a short, vicious slam from Clint's knee. Once again, the man's air flowed out of him in a gasping rush and he crumpled over.

Clint was just about to let the man go when he saw the two men in front of him fly out of that stall. One of them came out on his own two feet and he twisted around to take a shot at Clint. The other came out backward and had gotten all of his momentum by absorbing a savage kick from an angered mule.

The man who didn't just get his chest caved in meant to fire a round at Clint. He stared through the growing flames coming from the hay bale and shattered lantern, only to find himself looking at one of his own partners.

Another shot cracked through the air. For a moment, the man at the stall thought it might have been something popping in the fire, but he changed his mind when he felt the pain lance up along his whole left side. In an instant, that pain flared up and he felt the blood start to flow from the fresh wound that had just been torn through his leg.

When he put his hand down to cover the painful spot, the man let out an agonized grunt and dropped over onto the floor. The gun went off in his hand as he hit the floor. Rolling onto his side, he was just in time to see Clint rushing toward him with his Colt held at hip level.

Clint had dropped the man he was using as a shield after cracking him behind the ear using the handle of his Colt. From there, he meant to get to the only remaining threat he could see before he was forced to shoot again. In his mind, he had his steps planned out so he could plant one foot and use his other to kick the other man in the jaw.

Unfortunately, things didn't always go according to plan. That is, it was unfortunate for the man who was quick enough to get his gun up and take aim before Clint could get close enough to knock him out.

If he had another second, Clint would have been able to get where he wanted to go and not have to kill another man. His steps didn't seem to come fast enough, however, and with his aching bones and lungs full of smoke, he knew the only thing he would do if he waited another second was catch a bullet.

So, with no other alternative, Clint snapped his hand forward and aimed the Colt as if he was pointing his finger. One pull of a trigger was all it took for him to send a round into the heart of his target, causing the man on the floor to drop his gun a hairbreadth away from firing it himself.

Clint still ran forward, ignoring the billowing smoke and crackling fire. Instead of kicking anyone into unconsciousness, he used that momentum to stomp on the flames before they could spread past the front of the charred hay bale.

TWENTY-TWO

Clint was actually surprised that he was able to get the fire out as quickly as he did. That was the one part of his improvised plan that had worried him the most. If he'd been caught in a hail of bullets or trapped inside a burning barn, he would have been just as dead. Also, despite the fact that he'd been greeted with an ambush, Clint wasn't the type of man to let other human beings die in a fire.

There were some things that just defined the difference between self-defense and outright cruelty. Clint showed his true colors by gritting his teeth through the burning of flames licking his boots and the smoke choking his every breath while he stomped out the last of the fire. He then dragged the men out that were still breathing yet unable to get out on their own.

Just for good measure, Clint went back into the stable and climbed up into the loft to check and see if there was anyone he'd missed. He'd managed to find another lantern that hadn't been lit, and carried that in one hand as he hung onto the ladder with the other. The moment he poked his head up onto that upper level, Clint spotted a trace of motion in the thick shadows.

"Come on out of there," Clint warned even though he

couldn't make out much more than a rough shape. "It's all over."

He gave it a few more seconds before raising his voice again.

"When I leave this place, I'll just drop this lantern behind me. I might as well, since all you men are so intent on killing me."

Even though he hadn't really expected that last threat to get any results, Clint was still angry that he had to climb up the rest of that ladder when he was hoping to just take a look from where he was. With one more gunman left, however, Clint couldn't exactly just turn his back on the other man and leave.

Drawing in a deep breath, Clint gathered his strength and poured all of it into his legs. With all that steam built up inside him, Clint jumped up the remaining rungs and threw himself into that loft headfirst. As he was diving into a mess of straw and scraps of broken wood, he saw a flash of gunfire in the corner of his eye and heard the hiss of lead whip past him.

Clint twisted in midair and landed on one side. Not wanting to start another fire when he'd been lucky enough to put out the first, he strained to keep the lantern off the floor even as his ribs pounded against the boards. He landed with a jarring thump and skidded for less than a foot. When he came to a stop, Clint brought his Colt around and aimed the best he could.

The man who'd been hiding up there pulled his trigger again, but was in too much of a hurry to adjust his aim for Clint's fall. The second bullet flew as high as the first, also missing Clint by a mile.

Clint squeezed his trigger, sending what he knew to be his sixth shot into the shadows. The round may not have been a hit, but it served its purpose by causing the other man to pull back before taking more careful aim. Clint didn't like wasting a shot, but wasn't too comfortable with lying there and waiting for the other man to come to his senses and actually aim for a change.

He heard a grunt, which could have been because of a wound or just from the shock of a near miss. Whichever it was, Clint decided to play what little of an advantage he'd made and pushed himself up onto his feet. If his bones had been aching before, they were crying for mercy after his rough landing from a few moments ago. Clint didn't have time to ache just then. He was too busy fighting for his life.

Clint wanted to sound angry, and didn't have to do too much acting to get the proper snarl in his voice. "All right, you asshole, since you can't shoot for a damn, then maybe you'll know when to quit."

Now that he was on his feet and had run forward a few steps, he could easily make out the shape of the remaining man trying to scoot back behind a medium-sized crate. Even in the shadows, Clint could see the other man's eyes were wide as saucers as he stared down the Colt's barrel.

Clint knew his cylinder was carrying nothing but spent shells. The main thing, however, was if the other man knew that same thing.

"All right then," Clint said, fixing his eyes on the other man and then down at the gun, which was still smoking in that one's fist. "Looks like we've got ourselves a nice little standoff here."

The other man sucked in a breath and tried to look like he wasn't deathly afraid. He wasn't doing a very good job. "You've been shooting back and forth this whole time. I bet you're out of rounds in that gun."

"Am I?" Clint put on an overly exaggerated thinking expression. He then took a moment to move his lips and other hand as though he was counting silently to himself.

Clint knew well enough that he was out of ammo and at that range, even the sloppiest of shots would be able to put him down. Depending on how the situation played out, he could either sweep up the last attacker or be shot dead on the spot.

Every moment he bought by silently counting to himself gave the other man a chance to get a better look at the Colt, which was staring right back at him. Finally, Clint shrugged and gave up on his pretend arithmetic. "You know something? I did do a lot of shooting and I can't recall if I reloaded or not somewhere along the line."

The other man started to smirk, but faltered when his eyes were drawn inevitably back to the Colt. In that instant, Clint knew the man in front of him was the one who wasn't sure how many shots were fired.

"I know I fired off five or six," Clint said. "I guess there's only one way to settle this for sure." With that, he steeled his expression and let his eyes turn ice cold. Clint then thumbed back the hammer just so the other man could get an earful of that distinctive, metallic click.

A heartbeat after the hammer snapped into place, the other man lost his remaining bit of self-control and pitched his gun away like a hot coal. His previous expression fell away like a sheet that had been pulled from a painting to reveal his true face, which was stark, pale terror.

"Don't shoot me," the other man begged. "Please. I'll go along to a jail or leave town or whatever you want, but please don't kill me."

Clint nodded and released the hammer so he could lower it onto what he knew to be an empty casing. "Now that's what I like to hear."

TWENTY-THREE

When he left the stable along with the man who'd come along as a willing prisoner, Clint noticed immediately that he was one man short. He'd been in a hurry to clear the stable and had left the unconscious gunmen outside, hoping they'd still be asleep when he got back. Everyone was accounted for except for the man he'd used as a shield. Apparently, he'd gotten a second wind and used it to scamper off.

Clint had found a coil of rope in the stable and tossed it over to the man he'd just convinced to leave the building. "Here. Use this to tie up your friends. Make it all in a nice, neat line for me."

The other fellow did as he was told, and then allowed Clint to wrap his own wrists together as well before sealing it all off with a solid knot.

"Where's the law in this town?" Clint asked.

The other man shook his head. "There ain't no regular law. Every so often a marshal comes through or someone can get word to a sheriff."

Clint wasn't too surprised by that, especially for a town the size of Mehlville Crossing. That did, however, leave him with a distinct problem since there were three men that needed a safe place to stay; namely a place behind bars.

Just as he started looking around for someone to ask for help, Clint spotted a slender figure leaning against the front of the hotel. Despite the darkness and the confusion of the last several minutes, there was no way Clint could possibly miss the attractiveness of that figure.

She wore clothes that were made to ride the trail, complete with thick cotton shirt and broken-in jeans. Long, dark hair flowed over her shoulders and was tussled by the passing breeze. She seemed to be watching Clint with amusement, and gave him a slightly playful smirk once she saw that she'd finally been noticed.

"I don't suppose you'd know where men like this would be kept, do you?" Clint asked, giving the rope in his hands a tug to jostle the prisoners.

She leaned forward and craned her neck to get a better look. "If I were you, I'd say that barn was about right."

"Can't say as I disagree, but these fellas need something a little more secure. Any other ideas?"

"No, but I think I know someone who could help." With that, she reached out to knock loudly a few times on the front door of the hotel.

The door was pulled open immediately and Anne poked her head outside. "Is the shooting over? Is it safe?"

"It's safe," the dark-haired woman said. "Someone out here could use some advice."

The older woman seemed afraid at first, but when she saw Clint standing in the street with the gunmen tied up behind him, she shuffled outside like she was greeting a genuine hero. "Mr. Adams! I'm so happy you weren't hurt! But you should be more careful. You could have been killed. Are you all right?"

"I'm a little rattled, but other than that not bad," Clint replied. "Could you tell me where troublemakers are usually kept in this town?"

"All the drunks and roughnecks are locked up in what used to be MacCreedy's smokehouse. I swear, if this whole town blew away in a twister, that smokehouse would still be there. I can show you there if you like."

"Just tell me where it is and I'll take them myself. No need to get you mixed up in this."

"That's so sweet of you. I'll let Mr. MacCreedy know you're coming and he'll bring out the keys so you can lock up those damn troublemakers."

"Much obliged."

Anne walked with quick, shuffling steps, and paused before she'd gone more than ten feet. "When I get back," she said to Clint, "I'm going to make you a nice big meal. No leftovers for someone like you, Mr. Adams. I'm going to recommend you for sheriff!"

Before Clint could say a word to that, Anne was already on her way. In her excitement, she'd neglected to give him the directions to the smokehouse, which had been his original reason for dragging her out of the hotel in the first place. The dark-haired woman noticed this as well, and laughed when Clint looked back her way.

"She's headed in the right direction," she told Clint. "Just walk that way and you'll see the smokehouse on your right before too long."

"Thanks," Clint said with a tip of his hat. "Is there some way I can thank you for your help?"

She nodded and turned to walk back into the hotel. "I'm sure I can think of something."

TWENTY-FOUR

The dark-haired woman had been absolutely correct. Not only could Clint spot the smokehouse from a ways off, but he could smell it after getting just a little bit closer. The men he was dragging behind him didn't have any fight left in them whatsoever, and even seemed glad once they could sit down inside the solidly built smokehouse.

As soon as he'd opened the door, Clint was overtaken by the smell of ham and sausage that still hung inside the makeshift jail after soaking into each brick wall. Anne waited nearby with another older gentleman, who was ready to lock the door once Clint tossed the prisoners inside.

Still holding the rope, Clint turned to the older man and asked, "Is it safe for me to take this off of them?"

The older man was lanky and wore a mustache that looked like a gray brush glued to his upper lip. That mustache only shifted slightly when he replied, "Sure, you can take that rope off. Better men than these three have tried to get out without any luck."

"Do you know these men?"

"Yeah," the older fella answered after a quick glance

at each face. "Can't say as I'll miss 'em once the law comes by to take them out of here."

Part of Clint wondered how the other man knew the prisoners and when the law would be coming through town. But that was a small part of Clint, which was easily overshadowed by the fatigue that had sunken into every joint and muscle. By the time he'd loosened the knots and reclaimed the rope, he didn't care about much of anything besides getting some food in his belly and a soft pillow under his head.

There was one more loose end to take care of before leaving the smokehouse, however. As soon as the door shut, Clint stepped up to it and peered through a small, square window that had been fitted with a single, thick iron bar. The last man he'd pulled out of the loft was staring back at him with tired defeat in his eyes.

"Hey," the prisoner said to Clint. "I got to know."

Clint smirked, drew his Colt, and then opened the cylinder. One by one, the empty shell casings were dumped into his hand so he could hold them up to the window. "Guess I needed to reload after all."

Although the other two prisoners hadn't known what was going on at first, they were sharp enough to figure out that they'd been corralled and shut into a prison at the end of an empty gun. They looked over to the third man, who couldn't decide whether he was more angry at himself for being bluffed or for drawing attention to it in front of his partners.

Clint didn't care much, but was glad the man had asked the question. Seeing that look on the man's face was enough to put a smile onto his own.

"I heard there was quite a scuffle in bringing these cowboys in," the older man with the smokehouse keys said.

"It wasn't easy, but it's done. I'm heading back to the hotel, unless you need something else."

"No, not at all. You've done more in one night than the last slug who tried to act as law around here. If there's a reward coming for any of these men, I'll be sure you get it."

But Clint hadn't heard much of anything once he knew that there was nothing left for him to do. He gave the older man a wave and then started walking back toward the hotel. Anne was nowhere to be seen, so Clint walked on his own down the street until he got to the familiar doorway of the hotel.

The smell of burning wood and straw replaced the scent of smoked ham as Clint got closer to the stable. He took one last look inside the drafty building to make sure that Eclipse was safe in a stall and there were no more fires smoldering somewhere. With that done, he barely made it into the hotel before collapsing onto the first available chair.

It must have been instinct that led him to the proper place, because Clint found himself at the dining room table, which was already filling up with plates of beef and bowls of potatoes. Just when he'd pulled in a deep breath filled with all those delicious aromas, Clint saw the door to the kitchen swing open and Anne come in holding a basket full of biscuits.

"These were made just this morning, so they shouldn't be too bad," she told him while setting the basket on the table next to all the rest. "I heated up everything for you and if there's not enough, you just let me know."

"I'm sure there'll be plenty," Clint said. Although when he picked up a fork and put the first bite into his mouth, his stomach churned to make room for plenty more.

"I'll fetch you something to drink," Anne said. The moment those words were out of her mouth, she disappeared back into the kitchen.

Clint had to hold himself back from simply tearing into

the food like a savage, but he was too hungry to go over-board with politeness. Besides, there wasn't anyone around to watch him anyway. That thought was still fresh in his mind when Clint spotted a familiar figure easing around the corner from the front room.

"I didn't get much of anything to eat myself," she said in a smooth, seductive tone. "But something tells me Anne would chop the hands off of anyone who dared touch a scrap of this food she set out for you."

Clint waved toward the closest empty chair. "And something tells me that if I forgot, you'd be sure to remind me that I said I owed you something by way of thanks."

Not only did she walk up to the chair he'd offered, but after sitting down, she scooted a little bit closer to Clint. "I wasn't worried about that." Smirking, she added, "But I would have reminded you if need be."

The door to the kitchen swung open and the steps coming through stopped short. Clint didn't have to look behind him to know that Anne was standing in the doorway staring at the other seat that had been filled.

"I've got company for dinner," Clint said, nipping the inevitable scolding in the bud. "Would that be all right?"

"Anything you like, Mr. Adams. I'll fetch another plate, but after that I'm off to bed. This has been too much excitement for me in one night."

Clint gave her a warm, genuine smile. "Thanks, Anne. I really appreciate all of this."

"Think nothing of it, dear."

Anne brought back the plate as promised, and patted the dark-haired woman's hand after setting it down. "You just leave everything when you're done and I'll clean up in the morning." With that, she said her good-nights and headed for the stairs.

"I think I'll need something else from you before I let you take any of my food," Clint said with a bit of sternness in his voice.

The dark-haired woman looked at him, knowing he wasn't as angry as he sounded, but wary of what could be coming next. "What else do you need from me?" she asked.

Clint waited for a moment before stating his terms. "Your name. Mine is Clint Adams."

Laughing and extending her hand, she said, "I'm Megan Walsh."

Shaking her hand, Clint felt a surprising amount of strength in her grip. Even so, there was nothing masculine about her. Clint even found her strength and bearing very intriguing to say the least.

"Mind if I eat now?" she asked, keeping her eyes fixed on Clint's.

"Go right ahead."

Soft, red lips closed around her fork and she slid a bite of meat into her mouth. She rarely took her eyes from him, as though she was sizing him up every bit as much as he was taking in the sight of her.

TWENTY-FIVE

"If those were leftovers," Clint said while patting his stomach and trying to make it up the stairs, "then I'd be afraid to be around Anne's cooking when it's fresh out of the oven. I might just eat so much that I'd bust open."

Megan was behind Clint, and was having just as difficult a time making it up the stairs. "For a woman who's only got one more guest in here apart from us, she cooks for an army."

Once at the top of the staircase, Clint saw that there was only one lantern burning at the other end of the hall next to two open doors. The rest of the rooms were shut off and the entire second floor had the stillness of people trying to get their sleep.

"Come on," Megan said, taking hold of Clint's elbow and leading him to one of the rooms. "Before we wake somebody up."

As much as he wanted to get some sleep now that his belly was full, Clint wasn't about to argue with the beautiful woman pulling him toward her room.

Megan Walsh was tall and had a lithe, supple frame. She stood almost as tall as Clint, but didn't have a bit of the awkwardness that most taller women seemed to have.

When she moved, it was with a silent grace and not one of her steps made more than a whisper of noise. Long, black hair flowed down her back, swaying behind her like a cloak that reached down just far enough to brush the upper slope of her tight buttocks.

Although they seemed to be more tailored for a cowboy, the clothes she wore hugged her body to leave no doubt that she was anything but a cowboy. On the contrary, her slender hips and firm backside were accentuated by her jeans. Even her slightly baggy shirt couldn't hide the curve of her pert breasts.

As their meal had progressed, Clint had noticed that she'd watched him carefully and allowed her chair to drift slightly closer to his own. Afterward, she'd stayed close to him so that even when they'd gone upstairs, he could feel her presence as close to him as if they were lying in the same bed.

With that particular thought in mind, Clint found himself in her darkened room. With only the starlight and what little moonlight there was to aid him, he was still able to see the room was nothing short of a wreck. There were crumpled clothes lying here and there piled somewhat close to what appeared to be a carpetbag sitting in a corner.

The room was small, but had the cozy feel of a space that was in someone's home as opposed to one in an average hotel. Most of the space was taken up by a modest bed and a small chest of drawers. There was a little table with a washbasin, but that was it. Everything else in the room was obviously Megan's, and her fresh, vaguely sweet scent was heavy in the air.

Clint took all of this in within the space of a heartbeat. That was a habit that had become so natural after years of needing to survey his surroundings that he no longer even thought about it. At least that way, he could devote most of his attention to the finer things nearby.

"Here we go," Megan said, glancing back over her shoulder with a toss of thick, wavy hair. "I think some fresh air will do us both some good."

Letting his eyes focus on Megan's inviting curves, Clint allowed himself to be dragged toward a narrow rectangular window, which led outside much like the one in his hotel room in Plattsmith. Unlike that hotel, however, this balcony wasn't much more than a ledge intended for plants and such.

Megan still had hold of Clint's arm and after she'd stepped outside, she pulled him out along with her. She kept tugging until Clint's body was snug against her own, and they were both in the cold grip of the nighttime breeze.

"Mmmm," Megan purred softly while shifting her body against him. "This is nice."

The balcony was slightly bigger than it looked, and there was just enough room for both of them to stand there and admire the night sky. Clint took a moment to let the scenery soak in and when he was done with that, he concentrated on how good it felt to be pressed up against Megan's inviting body.

It seemed that she was thinking the same thing because she let out another contented sigh. "I love this time of year," she said. "It's so much nicer being cold than hot. If I had my way, I'd be further north where I could feel the real cold of winter."

"Really? How much further north were you thinking?"

"Maybe Canada."

Clint shivered and made a sound of his jaw chattering that got a little laugh out of her. "Makes me cold just thinking about Canada in the winter," he said. "So what brings you to Ohio?"

Although she started to answer, she stopped short and turned around to look at him. "I just remembered that I only met you a few hours ago."

"Do I frighten you?"

"No, but I'm not sure I can trust myself around someone like you."

"Afraid I'll take advantage of a well-meaning woman like yourself?"

Megan laughed once and turned back around to look at the street. "Try turning that around and you'd be a lot closer to what I had in mind. Either way, I think you should probably go." Shifting against him, Megan found a comfortable spot and then actually tightened her grip on the arm that was around her. "Well, pretty soon anyway."

When the breeze came by, Clint could feel the bite of cold chew through his layers of clothing as though they weren't even there. The night air went straight down to his bones and just when he felt a shiver coming on, he felt some of the warmth from Megan's body soak into his like a welcome wave of sunlight.

He knew exactly how contented she felt because he felt the same way. Despite the cold and despite all the unpleasantness that had brought him to Mehlville Crossing, Clint was glad to be there at that point in time. He swore silently to himself, however, when he thought about those reasons for him coming to town.

"You're right," he said regretfully. "I should be going."

There was a killer still loose in town, after all.

TWENTY-SIX

The burn of whiskey was fresh in the back of Drogan's throat. Before it could fade too much more, he brought a bottle up to his lips and tipped it back. Liquor swirled inside the glass like a miniature squall before sloshing through the opening and draining down his throat.

It tasted bitter at first. Hell, whiskey never tasted good. Like any good drunk, he gritted his teeth through that bitter taste until the real payoff arrived. That burn ignited inside him, like someone had dropped a match onto his tongue so the flame could trace a hot path all the way down into his gullet.

Once the burn pulsed through him, Drogan felt his muscles relax and the tension inside him finally taper off. He let out the breath he'd been holding, even though he knew all that tension would return in a matter of seconds before he took another pull from the bottle.

Normally, he would be drinking in a saloon. Especially when he was in a new town, Drogan preferred to drink where he could watch the locals and pick out which ones were the bulls among all the cattle. To any man interested in death as a living, the saloons were the hub of any town. They were the

105

wilds within civilization and a place for true predators to stalk their prey.

Drogan felt as though he'd grown up in saloons, and had been to so many that they all seemed to blend into a flow of experience rather than standing apart as separate establishments in his mind. After using them as a place to do business for so long, he'd also come to regard them as his only true home.

But there were some times when even a man's home wasn't entirely safe. This was most definitely one of those times. Drogan figured Clint Adams would follow him, but had hoped for a better head start out of Plattsmith. Apparently, The Gunsmith was a fair tracker after all.

Once the burn of whiskey started to fade and the swirl in his head slowed to a halt, Drogan let his head fall forward and felt the tension come back into him.

"Who the hell am I fooling?" he thought. "A blind man could have followed me here."

The truth of the matter was that Drogan had hoped for some peace and quiet so he could finish his business. With Adams around, he wouldn't be as free to do what he needed to do. There was even the distinct possibility that he might not get it done at all.

"No," Drogan snarled. "It will get done." When he spoke, he slammed his bottle down onto the little table in front of him for emphasis. Even though there was nobody else in the room with him, Drogan stared straight ahead as if he was holding someone else's gaze.

"I can't move on like I used to," he said to nobody. "I'm too old for that. I'm too . . . too damn tired."

Those last three words had come out of him unexpectedly. During the course of his life, being too tired to move was a luxury he simply could never afford. If he wasn't on the run from his father, or the asshole kids that had tormented him in his youth, he'd been running from the law or some goddamn bounty hunter.

Being an outlaw meant being both the wolf and the rabbit. With all the differences those animals had, they were both runners. Being still meant being dead, and that was just as true for an outlaw as it was for a rabbit.

Having to admit that he was too tired to keep moving was like having to admit that he could no longer lift his pistol. It was asking a wolf to pull out its own teeth, and that simply wasn't going to happen.

Drogan lifted the bottle to his lips, tipped it back, and kept pouring even after he'd swallowed three entire mouthfuls. The fire blazed inside him, and the entire room began to tilt at odd angles around him. When his vision started to split, Drogan lowered the bottle and kept the full load of whiskey in his mouth without swallowing.

Slowly, the liquor trickled down his throat. It was right about then that he realized he felt lower than the bottom of the bottle in his hand. Throughout the years, he'd soaked up enough whiskey to keep him from thinking about the sins he'd committed.

It had started out as a way to build up his courage. Then it had dulled the pain. Now, it was the only way he could sleep at night without being awakened by the screams of the ghosts that haunted nearly every one of his waking moments.

The bottle slipped from his fingers and he slumped back into his chair. His head lolled back and for a moment, he thought he was going to pass out altogether. In fact, he hoped he was going to pass out because at least that way he could have gotten some rest.

But instead of slipping into unconsciousness, Drogan merely lost his ability to move while the rest of him stayed awake so he could keep wondering what the hell he was doing. He was a known man. He was feared. There was a healthy price on his head, and he even had enough money stashed away to live the rest of his life comfortably.

Instead, he was in an empty, rented room, unable to move because of the poison coursing through his entire body. Just thinking about that was enough to start purging the whiskey from his blood. It wasn't a miracle, but just a product of having finished off more bottles over the years than he could count.

The whiskey simply wasn't effective any more.

What it all came down to was that Drogan hadn't gone to Plattsmith to drink. He hadn't come to Mehlville Crossing to hide out in some cheap back room.

He'd come all this way for a reason, and that reason was good enough to pass up an easier life north of the border. It was time to finish his business, but that didn't mean it was easy. All of Drogan's life had led up to this, but somehow he still didn't feel ready for it.

The sad fact was that he didn't have much time left to finish this job and if it didn't get done, the rest of his life wouldn't mean a damn thing.

Maybe he did need some more whiskey.

TWENTY-SEVEN

Not only had Anne kept her word by whipping up a fantastic dinner, but her breakfast promised to be just as good. When Clint woke up the next morning, it was to the smell of frying bacon and coffee. Before he knew what he was doing, he was out of bed, dressed, and headed down the stairs.

It was just past dawn when he sat down to the table. It wasn't until a few moments after that when he realized that he no longer had the dining room to himself. Looking around, Clint spotted at least a dozen people either sitting around the table or walking in and out of the lower floor. Now, Clint could see how she could stay in business with only a few rooms to rent at a time.

"Good morning, Mr. Adams," Anne said, spotting him immediately even though he was practically swallowed up by everyone else around him. "Sit down and I'll bring you a plate."

He started to respond, but saw that he was already too late. Anne had turned and shuffled back into the kitchen. Looking first to his left and then to his right, Clint glanced around for a familiar face. He didn't have any luck. Fortunately, a familiar face found him.

109

"Well there you are," a soft, welcome voice said from behind Clint's chair. "I had you pegged for the late-riser sort."

"Sometimes I am, Megan. But that's only when I've had a particularly busy night."

She stepped around and pulled a seat up next to him. "After nearly getting yourself shot and burned down, you still don't consider that a busy night?"

"Not as busy as it could have been. Speaking of busy, I'd say we're pretty lucky to have found somewhere to sit."

"There were a few folks who tried to take your seat before you came down, but Anne scared them off. You mind if I ride your coattails one more time?"

"You can ride anything you'd like."

She let that one lay right where it was, only giving him a smirk as a reply. Clint's food came out first, and Megan got her plate soon after. Although the food was fantastic, the dining room only got more crowded as more people came in to eat and more, smaller tables were set up to accommodate them.

With a full belly, Clint pushed away from the table and headed outside. The instant he stood up, someone else descended into his chair like a vulture waiting for a sick cow to tip over. Clint took a deep breath of fresh morning air, and was forced to step even further away from the hotel when another couple wanted to get inside.

Glancing across the street, Clint saw that the stable was a little the worse for wear, but was still standing. In the daylight, he could now see that the structure was even more ramshackle than he'd thought the night before. The boards looked like they'd seen more than one fire even before the previous night's blaze. Each plank seemed ready to fall off the frame either from rot or poor crafts-manship.

Clint had been in enough boom towns to recognize a

hasty construction job when he saw one. In fact, even though Anne's hotel looked sturdier than the stable, it didn't appear entirely permanent either. A couple steps into the street and then a couple steps along the road was all it took for Clint to get a better look at Mehlville Crossing as a whole.

More than just a quaint name, the town literally wasn't much more than the crossing of two somewhat major streets. The boardwalks were rickety, and he counted no more than eight real buildings in sight. Despite all that, the place seemed to be filled with people. Part of that was because of the cramped quarters, but another part came from the fact that there truly were a large amount of bodies crammed into a small amount of civilization.

Of course, those two factors weren't exactly new either. Clint had seen them come into play enough times to know what resulted from that mixture.

Blood.

If it didn't come from angry men punching each other, it came from the gunshots that were sure to erupt once too many wandering souls got too close together for too long. Towns like Mehlville Crossing might not have seemed much like towns, but they were the core of a gunfighter's career. It was places like that where men would go who not only thrived on blood, but practiced the craft of drawing it.

Now that he'd gotten a good look at it, Clint knew the place was perfect for someone like Two-Cent Drogan to go if he was seeking comfort. Mehlville Crossing may not have been around when Drogan was cutting his teeth, but it had to feel like home away from home.

Clint let all of that sink in as he turned back around toward the hotel. He was just in time to spot Megan as she walked out and headed straight for him.

"I didn't mean to leave you there by yourself," Clint

said. "But I didn't want to deprive Anne of any paying customers."

"That's all right. I couldn't hear myself think in there anyway. You're moving kind of funny. Were you hurt last night?"

Clint hadn't realized he was moving any differently, but now that she'd mentioned it, he was still feeling the effects of last night's tussle. "I guess I am still a little banged up. Not as young as I used to be, I guess."

She smiled and then ran her hand over his shoulder. "You look like you're in fine shape to me. But if you were expecting a smooth stay and a quiet night's sleep, you came to the wrong town."

"I found that out myself. The hard way."

"So why did you come here?" Megan asked, her eyes narrowing slightly as she watched him. "It doesn't look like you were passing through or you'd already be gone."

"I've got some business here."

"What kind of business?"

It was bad enough that Clint had been pulled into whatever drama Two-Cent had been staging. He didn't want to drag anyone else in as well.

"It's my business," was all Clint said.

Short, sweet, and just a little rude. Megan got the message.

"All right then," she said. "I'll just leave you to it."

TWENTY-EIGHT

Clint's gut instinct had been that he would find Drogan in Mehlville Crossing. That, along with the fatigue of a long day's ride, had been more than enough reason to stay put. Now that he'd gotten a better feel for the town in general, Clint knew that his instincts had once again been proven right.

The place just felt like a fight waiting to happen. If he'd doubted that at first glance, being ambushed while trying to put Eclipse away for the night would settle the matter. Now he walked the streets, both of them, and soaked up the air, which seemed to crackle with aggression.

Most of the folks seemed friendly enough. Those were the ones that had a good reason for being there and not moving on to a bigger or better town. Those were the shopkeepers, blacksmiths, bakers, and other business owners. Although they didn't give Clint a reason to fret, their own faces seemed haunted by the rest of the folks that made up the population.

Those belonged to the dregs that floated into places like that the way refuse collected at the end of a river. As he walked down the street, Clint met up with twice as

many of those bloodthirsty stares as he did friendly faces.
In fact, the more he walked, the less friendly the other
faces became. That was probably due to the small crowd
that had gathered behind him.

As he kept moving, Clint could feel the other eyes on
his back, but only took a few quick glances over his
shoulder. Every time he looked, he saw more bodies behind him, until the sound of all those boots started to ring
through his ears. Finally, Clint hopped onto the battered
boardwalk and came to a quick stop.

When he turned around for a better look, Clint saw
that none of the men who'd been following him bothered
to cover up what they were doing. In fact, they stood there
looking at him like he was the one who was trespassing
on their territory.

Clint looked at each man in turn. Although each of
them seemed to think they were tougher than worn
leather, not one of them gave Clint a reason to worry. All
of them together, on the other hand, was another story
entirely.

Although he wasn't an outlaw gunman, Clint knew
their rules well enough. They were similar to pack animals, and the struggle for dominance was at the core of
their very souls. With this in mind, Clint steeled his eyes
and started walking straight toward the group of men.

They saw him coming, and a few of them even seemed
to be looking forward to getting within arm's reach of
him. That attitude changed, however, when Clint kept
right on walking until they were forced to step aside.

It was a simple game, bordering on childish. But Clint
was dealing with a simple mentality, and could feel that
he'd scored something of a victory over the ones who
stepped aside. By wearing an open challenge on his face
and letting his hand drift toward his gun, Clint laid out
the rules for their little game.

Every man he pushed aside meant Clint was taking

another step up in the pecking order. The men who did move tried to keep their chins up, but there was a definite change in their manner, which didn't start changing back until they got close to the others once again.

Clint parted the group until he came to the very back. Standing directly in front of him was a sight that genuinely surprised Clint. It was one of the men who'd ambushed him in the stable the previous night. Only this time, he wasn't showing the first sign of weakness.

"I remember you," Clint said, smiling. "I almost missed you, though. Maybe it's because you looked so much different when I was tossing you around like a rag doll."

When Clint had last seen that man, he'd used him for cover and thrown him aside when he was done. Thinking back to that and hearing Clint speak was enough to bring an angry twitch to the corner of the man's mouth and a cold look to his eyes.

"Yeah," the man said without a trace of goodwill in his smirk. "That's real funny. There seem to be a lot of funny people coming through here. Of course," he added, turning to look at the others gathering around him, "whether or not you leave this town is up to me."

"Up to you? I hope you're not relying on these others to back you up. They seemed kind of skittish."

"Yeah, well, they don't jump unless I tell 'em to. And if you want me to tell 'em, then you're headed the right way."

Without showing weakness, Clint said, "I'm not looking for trouble."

"What are you looking for?"

"What about Two-Cent Drogan? You ever heard of him?"

The other man nodded. "I heard of him. If you're looking to find him, you might want to try the graveyard outside of town. Oh, and you might want to bring a shovel."

TWENTY-NINE

Drogan wasn't dead.

Clint didn't buy that line of bull for a second. The only reason for that lie at all was to allow Clint to walk away without the other man compromising his pride in front of the others. Since he wasn't there to get in a small-town pissing contest, Clint let the other man talk tough and he left.

None of the others said a word to him as he left. They weren't that stupid.

But that still left Clint with his original problem. Drogan was still out there and Clint still needed to find him. With all he knew about the mind of a gunfighter, Clint headed for the one place that he knew Drogan would show up sooner or later.

The saloon.

The only reason it had taken him that long to get there was because Clint wanted to allow Two-Cent enough time to feel secure where he was. Tracking the other man to yet another town simply was not on Clint's list of fun things to do.

The only saloon in town was a long building that reminded Clint of a ranch house, at the opposite end of the street from Anne's hotel. The place wasn't far from the smokehouse where Clint's attackers from the night before were cooling their heels, and they were all still in there when he stopped by to check on them.

With the rest of his business squared away, Clint walked to the saloon and stepped inside. As he moved through the front door, he prepared himself for anything and everything. His hand stayed far enough away from his Colt to appear non-threatening, yet stayed close enough to allow him a quick draw if the need came up.

The saloon had no upper floors, and did not have a sign nailed out front or painted on any window. All Clint had needed was the scent of stale liquor and the sound of rowdy voices to guide him to the proper place. Now that he was there, he kept his eyes peeled for Drogan.

Knowing how tough old habits were to break, Clint started his search at the back of the saloon. His eyes only had to sweep that area once before they hit pay dirt. He felt a cold vise tighten around his stomach as he headed past the bar and toward Drogan's seat.

The older man had looked up as soon as Clint stepped inside, and had yet to take his eyes off him. As Clint drew closer, Drogan leaned back in his chair and displayed the specially made gun hanging at his side. "I knew you'd come, Adams. I thought it'd be sooner, though."

"I was a little busy last night."

"Yeah. I heard. Nasty business. And here I thought I was supposed to be the bad element around here."

"What the hell are you doing here?" Clint asked.

"Funny. I was about to ask you the same thing."

"You don't have anything to prove."

Drogan leaned forward and placed both hands flat upon the table. "That's where you're wrong. A man like you doesn't have anything to prove. A man like myself has got nothing else to do with his life than prove himself. When I stop proving my worth, I get shot down by some punk kid out to put a notch on his belt or just get some blood on his hands."

"You don't have to stay in this life, Drogan. You could always move on."

"You see? You're not so thickheaded after all. That right there was the idea I've had for a while now. I've got enough tucked away to retire on, and I even got the spot picked out for me to plant my ass onto a rocker and sleep through my last days on this earth."

"Then why not make that happen? It would be a whole lot easier than . . . well . . . whatever it is you think you're doing."

Drogan shook his head. The stench of whiskey coming from him was so powerful that it seemed as though he'd been soaked in the stuff. His eyes were clear, however, and his occasional movements were steady. "I think I'm doing what's got to be done."

Clint watched the other man as he spoke and even as he moved. There was something about Drogan that made Clint pause before simply confronting him about the men he'd shot or even the threats he'd made against Clint. Drogan's eyes had a look about them that reminded Clint of a wounded old wolf.

There was hurt in there, but danger as well.

Before he could press Two-Cent any further, Clint was interrupted by the sound of the front door being kicked in so hard that he could also hear the distinctive crack of splintering wood.

"There they are!" came the voice of the one man who hadn't backed down from Clint outside. "Both of the pains in my ass together in one place. Ain't this just perfect?"

"Do me a favor," Drogan said to Clint after giving the man who'd just stormed inside only a passing glance. "Whatever you want from me or whatever questions you wanted to ask, I'll go along with them just so long as you do something for me in return."

Clint nodded once and said, "That depends on what it is."

"That loudmouthed boy over there. The one by the door. His name's Brody and I want a crack at him."

"Look," Clint said, shaking his head, "I'm not about to stand by and help you—"

"You won't have to help me do anything. Just don't hold me back and for the love of God, don't stand in my way."

There was something else in Drogan's voice that made Clint sit up and take notice. It was something that he hadn't heard before, and sure as hell didn't think he'd ever hear from the old gunfighter.

Drogan was pleading with him.

Not in so many words, but in the tone of his voice as well as the intense emotion in his eyes. He was pleading with Clint as much as he could allow himself to plead, even going so far as invoking the Almighty himself.

Clint couldn't believe what he was doing when he nodded to Drogan and stepped aside. Part of him was responding to Two-Cent as one human being to another in crisis. The other part of him just wanted to see what would happen next.

THIRTY

Brody was the type of man who was instantly forgettable after a first glance. Even though Clint had been closer to him than any of the others at that ambush in the stables, he'd have a hard time picking out Brody's face in a crowd. Even now, with Brody drawing all the attention to himself, Clint still had a hard time believing this was the same man as before.

Almost as tall as Clint and slightly thinner, Brody sneered at both Clint and Drogan as though he didn't know which one to tear apart first. "I'll deal with you later, old man," Brody said to Drogan. "Right now, I want to deal with that arrogant piece of horse shit standing there next to you."

Everyone in the saloon looked over at Clint, waiting for him to respond to Brody's insult. Clint, however, was the calmest one in there. He was beyond anger and back in his normal state of mind where he was thinking clear as crystal.

Without allowing himself to be riled by the taunting words, Clint shrugged and stepped aside. He wasn't as nonchalant as he appeared, however, and prepared himself to launch into motion at the first sign it was needed.

Drogan not only seemed relaxed as well, but he appeared to be a man completely in his element. Clint could even feel the easing of tension from where he was standing.

"You want to deal with me?" Drogan asked. "Then you can do it outside. I need a smoke."

"No!" Brody snarled. "I'll do it—"

But Drogan had already moved past him and was headed for the front door. Although Brody still had things to say, he wasn't about to say them to someone's back. Letting out his breath in an angry hiss, he followed in Drogan's footsteps and charged out after the older man.

"Nobody turns their back on me, old man! Not unless they got a death wish."

Now standing at the opposite side of the street, Drogan stopped and spun around to face Brody. There was more life in his face than Clint had ever seen. Clint hadn't known the older man for very long, but the difference was more than enough to catch his attention.

Brody and the other men with him had come outside as well. Seeing that he'd been overlooked for the moment, Clint brought up the rear so he could keep his eye on everyone.

"Here," Drogan said sharply. "You want to keep talking?" With his eyes fixed on the younger man, Drogan reached into his breast pocket and removed a cigarette that he'd rolled earlier. He had a match out and lit it before Brody got up the nerve to talk again.

"I told you when you rode into town, old man. We don't take to no gunmen in Mehlville Crossing."

"Ain't that the pot calling the kettle black?"

After taking a moment to try and figure out what that meant, Brody only made himself more frustrated and said, "I call it whatever the hell I want. Maybe I should give you some time with your friend there so he can tell you how we treat unwelcome visitors here."

Drogan glanced over to where Clint was standing. When he looked back to Brody, he was wearing a sly grin. "I heard your men were stomped pretty good last night. The ones that lived are still sleeping it off in the smokehouse, aren't they?"

That got Brody so mad the younger man started to shake.

"And you," Drogan went on to say, pushing Brody even further, "were smacked around like a little bi—"

"That's it!" Brody said, unable to hold on to even a shred of self-control. "Draw that fuckin' gun of yours or I'll burn you down where you stand!"

Drogan's smile broadened just a little bit more. The change was so subtle that most anyone watching would have missed it. But Clint wasn't just anyone and he sure didn't miss a thing. He recognized what Drogan was doing as soon as Two-Cent had started verbally baiting his younger opponent. Just like in gambling, if someone allowed themselves to be rattled by words, they paid by sacrificing their concentration.

A fight was a kind of gamble, but the stakes were much higher. Therefore, if an experienced fighter could crack his opponent's will before a punch was thrown or a shot taken, he won himself a hell of an advantage. Drogan had just gained that advantage, and Clint had to admit it was interesting to watch a master at work.

"All right then," Drogan said calmly. "If that's what you want. Let's do this and get it over with."

Brody wanted it all right, but Drogan wanted it more. The fact that the older man didn't show it made Brody feel cocky. Clint shook his head at that, chalking up another small victory for Two-Cent.

Strutting into the street, Brody tossed his jacket open and flexed his hand over the butt of his holstered pistol. All the while, he smiled and glanced about at the folks watching him. He nodded to them like an actor romancing a crowd before finally turning his attention back to Drogan.

In contrast to the younger man's display, Drogan kept his distance from Brody without a flourish. He side-stepped to a spot in the middle of the street without once taking his eyes away from Brody. He wound up facing the saloon as well as Brody with his back to Anne's hotel in the distance.

"You sure you want to do this?" Drogan asked, masterfully playing on Brody's foul temper.

"There ain't no reason to hold off, is there?" Brody shot back. "First you and then," he added, pointing to Clint, "him."

"We'll see."

Drogan lowered his chin just enough so his eyes were staring level at Brody. The younger man seemed about ready to bust out of his skin, but was forcing himself to calm down so he could think. Clint figured the advantage was still with Drogan, but Two-Cent wasn't the one who had a half-dozen or so buddies standing by ready to back him up.

"Hold it!" came a voice from further down the street.

Clint as well as everyone else there turned to look at who was shouting for them to stop. There were two men walking at a quick pace toward the saloon. Both of them were buckling on gun belts and both of them probably still smelled like the inside of a smokehouse.

THIRTY-ONE

Both of the new arrivals were glaring at Clint, stalking toward him with bad intentions written all over their faces.

"That son of a bitch right there needs to pay for what he done."

Drogan spoke up quickly before Clint could do a thing. "Keep quiet, boy, before you get another beating tossed your way."

Still fuming, the released prisoner shifted his eyes toward Drogan. "What did you say?"

"You heard me. That is, unless your ears got smoked in there along with the rest of the bacon."

That got a laugh from the crowd. The sound rippled through and was quickly silenced, but it definitely had an effect on its two intended targets. Both of the prisoners squared their shoulders with Drogan and stepped up to stand at either side of Brody.

"How about you let us take this old man out for ya, Brody? After that, we get first shot at that other one over there."

Brody narrowed his eyes as he stared at Drogan, but eventually shot a quick glance over to the men on either side of him. "Why not?" he said. "You two were stupid enough to get your asses brought in the other night, so you might as well work it off. And if you get yourselves shot in the bargain, I'm rid of you for good."

Now smiling smugly, Brody stepped back and then walked to the other side of the street. He was careful to position himself well away from both Clint and Drogan so he could watch them both. It seemed as though he'd gotten some self-control back after all.

Clint watched this entire scene play itself out in front of him. On the one hand, there was Drogan, who was acting both in and out of control at the same time. On the other hand, there was Brody, who'd somehow gotten everyone in the crowd to fear him. Of course, Clint noticed the locals had started off plenty scared of Brody anyway. Why they were scared was something he intended on finding out.

For the moment, Clint settled with what was taking place presently. It didn't appear as though he was meant to step in just yet, so he hung back and waited for an opportunity to present itself.

Squinting at Drogan, the prisoner who'd been doing all the talking sneered and spit on the ground. "Didn't you get the message we sent you before, old man? I know we told you to get your wrinkled ass out of town, so why are you still here?"

The older gunfighter shrugged and said simply, "Does it matter?"

"No. I guess it doesn't."

After that, everyone in the street knew there were no more words to be said. Everyone who wasn't involved in the exchange of words quieted down to the point where it seemed that they were holding their breath. Even Clint felt the change in the air as the moment between both men facing each other in the street stretched on for one eternity after another.

With each second that passed without a movement

from either man, Clint became more anxious for that movement to come. After everything he'd seen, he wasn't at all sure which one he thought might make the first move.

Drogan was the more experienced of the two, but he was drunk and possessed a certain sluggishness that went beyond what any alcohol might give him.

The other man was fighting mad and raring to go, but if he hadn't drawn by now, that meant he knew better than to jump the gun.

Both men stood facing the other. Their eyes were fixed and their hands were steady over the grips of their weapons. Brody and the rest of his men watched, but seemed content to let the fight play out rather than step in to tip the scales in either direction.

Of all the souls out there, Drogan's was the hardest for Clint to figure out. The older man always seemed ready to fight, but didn't have that dangerous aggression that was all over the faces of most killers. There was something deadly beneath his surface, however, much like a snake coiled just beneath a thick patch of grass.

The only sound that could be heard was the wind as it rolled down the street and tossed whatever loose refuse it could find. Drogan and his quarry eyed each other intently, waiting for the other to make a move or for a good reason to make it themselves.

Since there wasn't much new to see on the younger man's face, Clint focused his attention on Drogan. When he looked over to Two-Cent, he saw something that he hadn't been expecting. There was an emotion flickering across his face, but it came and went quicker than a snap of white through a red and orange fire.

If Clint had to guess he would say that, every so often, Drogan looked afraid of what was going to happen. The fear wasn't very strong, but it reflected an uncertainty that gunfighters like Two-Cent Drogan simply never had. That kind of uncertainty, after all, usually resulted in more dead gunfighters than old ones.

Seeing that made it even harder for Clint to figure out why Drogan had been acting the way he had. After all, Drogan had been the one goading Clint into a fight. He'd also been the one still gunning younger men down in fights just like this one. That should have led to a braver, more confident Luke Drogan, and not one who seemed nervous standing in front of a kid like this one.

There may have been more to these younger gunmen than met the eye, but Clint doubted it. He had exceptionally good eyes.

Like any other gunfight, it started in an instant and quickly exploded into a chaotic jumble of sights and sounds. Although Clint couldn't spot exactly what had set it off, he did see both men reach for their guns as though a silent signal had been given. Since he wasn't directly involved in the fight, it was difficult for Clint to read between the lines.

He could see more than enough, however, to tell that they both seemed to draw at approximately the same time. There was a crack of gunfire and a puff of smoke from Drogan's pistol, and when Clint looked over to the other man, he saw the blood spray still hanging in the air and a body falling toward the ground.

Another shot sounded off as the younger fighter squeezed his trigger out of nothing more than a jerk of muscles as his body convulsed with pain. There was another shot, but it sounded different than the first. That caused Clint to look back over to Drogan, who seemed startled by the sound of the shot himself.

Even with the unusual expression on his face, Drogan took another shot toward the younger man, who had already hit the dirt on his back. Two-Cent lifted his pistol and began to turn when his eyes fixed on one of the others that had been standing nearby.

By the time Clint looked to see who Drogan had spotted, the second man who'd spent the night in the smokehouse was twisting back at an awkward angle. The shot that had taken him down ripped through the air while the others were still echoing into the distance, making it so that nobody seemed to know where to look or when it was safe to peek out from beneath whatever cover they'd taken.

Clint was wrapped up in the chaos as well, but was much cooler under fire than most anyone else. Although he also found his eyes darting back and forth, he wasn't so rattled that he didn't notice a few very odd things.

First of all, Drogan seemed awfully disoriented for a man who'd just picked off two targets without much effort.

Secondly, Drogan's copper-plated .44 wasn't smoking after taking that most recent shot.

THIRTY-TWO

The echo of gunfire still rang up and down the street. People who'd been watching were ducking and stepping away to stay out of the line of fire, and even the group that had been backing the other two men was thinking twice on whether or not they wanted to push Drogan any further.

But to Clint, the picture wasn't entirely one of chaos. He'd been in enough scrapes like this one to keep from being rattled by the sights and sounds. Instead, he was watching closely enough to pick out a few things that didn't quite fit.

Smoke hung in the air like a thick blanket, but there still wasn't enough to match the number of shots fired. Clint glanced up and down the street until his eyes caught something very interesting indeed. There was more smoke, but it was rising in a place nowhere near the saloon. When he saw that, several other things finally fit into place.

Of course, that also gave rise to a whole other set of questions that needed to be answered. Before he could do any of that, however, there was still the small matter of a gunfight that needed to be concluded.

"Son of a bitch!" Brody screamed as he drew his gun and took aim at Drogan. "Somebody put this bastard down!" he shouted, waving his free hand toward Clint.

More gunshots cracked through the air, whipping the bystanders into even more of a frenzy. These next shots were taken in a panic, and not one of them came close to doing any real damage. Both Drogan and Clint kept their heads low and moved quickly toward some cover. Clint picked a spot behind a water trough, and dropped down to sit with his back against the wooden box. Drogan got himself to a post that was thick enough to cover a good amount of him.

Two of Brody's men got enough guts to start walking toward Clint, squeezing off rounds as they went. A pair of those shots whipped over Clint's head before the next one or two chewed into the trough dangerously close to where Clint was hiding.

With no other alternative open to him, Clint leaned around to look past the trough and pulled his trigger. The Colt barked once in his hand, sending a bullet through the air to punch a hole through one of his attackers' skulls.

Just as the second man was about to fire at him, Clint shifted his aim and squeezed off a shot. The other man was stopped dead in his tracks and spun in a tight quarter circle as the Colt's bullet tunneled through his heart and exploded out the other side.

With both of his most immediate concerns accounted for, Clint looked over to see how Drogan was doing. The older man was still standing calmly behind his post, leaning out every so often to take a shot. From what Clint could see, Two-Cent had yet to hit much of anything. As Clint was watching, he saw one of the men that had been charging toward Drogan keel over as a shot was fired right into his stomach.

The shot could barely be heard amid the ruckus of shouting voices and stray gunfire, but Clint had heard it all the same. It was strange, however, that Drogan seemed to have hit the man without even pointing his gun in that direction.

Like most other gunfights, it was over in hardly any time at all.

The shots tapered off to leave nothing but the screams of the bystanders and the groans of the wounded. Brody, along with a few of his men, had expended their ammunition and were scampering off in different directions.

Clint fired a round at them to speed their way, making certain to put the bullet close enough to put some wind in their sails without drawing blood. Once he was sure that the fight was over, he went to where Drogan was standing and holstered his Colt.

"You all right?" Drogan asked.

Clint nodded. "What about you?"

Two-Cent pulled in a breath and when he let it out, he seemed to shave ten years off his appearance. "Couldn't be better."

If Clint had any doubts about that, they were nearly dispelled when Drogan stepped away from the post he'd been using as cover and turned to face what remained of the crowd. Now that the shooting was over, the bystanders were drifting back to see who was left standing and what was going to happen next.

Drogan was right there to show them just who was left at the top of the mountain. Wearing a smile that stretched from ear to ear, he stood up tall and proud while walking into the middle of the street. From there, he walked over to each of the bleeding men lying on the ground and checked them one by one.

Clint got the distinct impression that Drogan didn't give a damn how the men were doing. Instead, the older gunfighter appeared to be posing with each one in turn just to give the crowd something to focus on. When he made his way back to the saloon, Drogan knew he had the undivided attention of every bystander there.

Suddenly, Clint could feel an excitement moving through the crowd like a ripple spreading over a pond. That excitement stemmed from the display Drogan put on as he spun his .44 over his trigger finger in a tight, quick circle. The copper plating glinted in the sunlight, making his display of dexterity truly a sight to behold.

Drogan spun that pistol forward and back. He spun it to one side and then the other before finally slapping it back into its holster with a flick of his wrist. When the crowd saw that, they practically exploded again. A few of them even started to applaud, but every last one of them wore an expression of genuine admiration.

Every last one of them, that is, except for Clint.

He watched the display with sheer disbelief. Only moments ago, Drogan had seemed half dead and even afraid. Now, he strutted like a victorious general returning to his hometown. The happier Drogan seemed, the more Clint knew something was out of place.

But he knew better than to try and get the answers from Two-Cent himself. Clint wanted to start out by finding out who was really responsible for the fancy shooting that had saved Drogan's ass.

THIRTY-THREE

During the fight, Clint's ears had picked up the sound of gunshots coming from somewhere other than the men in the street. What he'd heard had come from further down the street, which was the same place that he'd seen that other source of telltale smoke.

Where there was smoke, there was always fire. The old saying couldn't have been truer than it was that day. Only this time, the fire in question was gunfire.

It was a rare breed of men who could keep their calm under fire. Even soldiers got rattled because that was the most reasonable way to handle being the target of incoming bullets. If a man could keep his head, he could usually keep his life as well once the lead started to fly.

Although he was a drunk and off balance somehow, Drogan was one of the men who could maintain his calm under the worst of circumstances. Clint knew that well enough because he was also one of that rare breed of men. It was thanks to that calmness that Clint had been able to detect more than just the sound of roaring pistols from moments ago. And it was that calmness that led Clint straight back to the hotel, which was directly across the street from the stable that had almost been burnt down the night before.

He was thinking about that ability to keep his head clear under stressful circumstances because that was the very thing that would allow Drogan to get away with having someone else do his shooting for him. With everyone confused and worried for their lives, they wouldn't be in any condition to question why he wasn't the one to fire the shots for which he was taking credit.

It required a very level head indeed to spot the mistakes that Clint had seen in that gunfight. Now that he knew what he'd seen, however, Clint had an entirely different outlook on what had been driving him to look closer at Drogan as a man.

All this time, Clint had known that something just wasn't quite right about Two-Cent Drogan. He'd felt it during every meeting, and that feeling had only gotten stronger the more he was around the older man. Until this moment, Clint was starting to feel as if he might be going crazy since he was the only one who saw anything wrong at all.

But Clint knew he wasn't crazy. In fact, the closer he got to the hotel, the more he'd figured out about what was going on. Now, standing in front of the hotel, he got an even better idea of who was involved in this strange tale.

His eyes were sharp enough to know where he'd spotted that smoke, which had since dissipated to a barely visible mist. If he concentrated, he could still smell the distinctive, bitter scent of gunpowder hanging in the breeze. When he closed his eyes and pulled in a deep breath, Clint could still picture what he'd seen that had brought him all the way to this end of the street.

Ignoring the excited buzz in the air regarding the recent fight, Clint walked past the locals milling about outside and entered the hotel. There were even more folks talking about the fight in there, but he ignored them as well and walked straight for the stairs that led to the upper floor.

At the top of the steps, Clint took a moment to situate himself and imagine which direction faced toward and which direction faced away from the street. When he turned toward the part of the house facing the street, Clint was left with only two choices of rooms that had a view of the spot where Drogan had made his stand.

Clint's room wasn't one of those choices.

Megan's room, on the other hand, was another story entirely.

First, Clint marked the rooms in his mind, then headed down the stairs again. Before he needed to ask around about her, he spotted Anne shuffling in from the kitchen nervously wiping her hands on an apron wrapped around her waist.

"My goodness," Anne said. "You certainly bring about the excitement in this town, Mr. Adams."

"It seems like that sometimes. Can I ask you something?"

"Go right ahead."

"How many rooms do you have to rent in this place?"

Anne's smile dropped off her face and she took a quick breath. "Is there something wrong with yours? Are those mice back?"

"No, there's . . . wait. What mice?"

"Nothing." The smile came back, but wasn't quite as bright as before. "Why do you ask?"

"Just curious."

"There's four rooms upstairs, but only three of them are being rented right now. That includes yours, of course."

"Of course."

"Was that all you needed?"

One of the biggest and most basic skills for any poker player to have was the ability to keep anyone else from knowing what you thought were the most important plays of the game. In keeping with that, Clint kept a casual expression on his face as he said, "Actually there was something else. It's not that important, but it would really help me out."

Anne stepped aside as someone walked through the lobby on their way to the dining room. "Name it," she said.

"I left something with Megan Walsh."

"I see."

"Would it be possible for you to let me in her room really quickly so I could get it? I can't find her right now and it would really be helpful if I could just run in there really quickly."

The older woman looked concerned, and she fretted with her apron strings with nervous hands. "I really shouldn't. I'd hate to intrude on Miss Walsh."

"It would only take a moment, and you could even stand right there and make sure I don't step out of line."

"Oh, it's not that I think you would—"

"Great," Clint said, pouncing on Anne's gracious mood before it changed. "If we could do this right now, that would be perfect."

"I thought that . . . well, I still don't . . ." She paused and saw his beaming, expectant smile. Shrugging, Anne said, "All right, but you've got to be quick about it."

THIRTY-FOUR

It wasn't until Anne had unlocked the door and opened it for him that Clint realized he had to think of something to tell her if she asked what he was looking for. He figured it wouldn't exactly be the smartest move to tell her what he was truly after, so he needed a quick answer if the question ever came. Fortunately, the older woman trusted him enough to let him poke his nose around inside Megan's room a bit before she said anything.

Clint stepped into the familiar room and took a look around. Everything was as it had been the night before, with a few small exceptions. The bed was a little more rumpled and a few personal things were scattered about, but those could very well have been in the same place since Clint hadn't bothered memorizing their positions.

"What is it you're looking for?" Anne finally asked.

Clint had just stepped around the other side of the bed and was crouching down to look under it. "My watch," he said, giving her the first small item that came to mind. "It must've fell out of my pocket and the last time I remember looking at it, I was up here."

Anne's cheeks flushed as she thought about why Clint would have been in Megan's room, but she kept her opinions to herself. Her little bit of discomfort worked in his favor since Anne didn't seem anxious to pursue the matter much further.

"All right then," she said nervously. "Just be quick about it. If you don't find your watch now, I can always ask her about it when she gets back."

Clint's eyes snapped up and he suddenly realized he'd almost overlooked the most obvious thing. "Where is she, by the way?"

"You just missed her. She left right before you got here and it looked like she wasn't going to be back for a bit. That's why I let you up here in the first place."

There wasn't anything but dust under the bed, and to search the room any more thoroughly would have surely looked suspicious. Clint stepped over to the window and took a look outside. He'd seen the view before, but that had been in the dead of night. Now that he knew what to look for and had more light to aid him, Clint saw what he wanted right away.

The room had a perfect view right down the street toward the saloon. There were people still milling about, and even some cleaning up the mess that had been left behind from the gunfight, allowing Clint to get a good sample of what someone might have seen from this angle.

Sure enough, someone looking out from this window would have had Drogan's back to them at the start of the fight. In fact, now that he thought about it, Clint figured Drogan's back was facing this way throughout the entire fracas. Not only that, but the figures walking in the street stood out rather well.

As he thought of all that, Clint imagined the puff of smoke he'd seen coming from this spot. He pulled in a deep breath through his nose and caught the scent of burnt gunpowder still hanging in the air. Just to make sure, he leaned forward and took a look along the side of the hotel.

There was one more window directly next to Megan's

that opened onto the same balcony and had pretty much the same view. Seeing that, he suddenly realized that he couldn't be absolutely sure that puff of smoke had come from Megan's window or the one right next to it. Feeling that uncertainty made Clint uneasy.

No gambler liked being uncertain of anything. When Clint's life was on the line, that was doubly so.

"Mr. Adams," Anne said, interrupting his train of thought. "I really think you should come out now."

Clint pulled himself inside and shut the window. "Of course. Sorry about that. I was just wondering if there was anyone in the room next door. This is one hell of a nice view."

Letting out a relieved breath once Clint was out of the room so she could lock the door up once again, Anne said, "That room is occupied, but I don't think it's for much longer. Would you like me to check on it for you?"

Clint gave her a disinterested shrug even though the possibility of a third player in the game could change a whole lot. "Sure," he said. "It wouldn't be much trouble for me to drag my things across the hall."

"All right then. I'll take a look for you."

Anne walked down the hall and went down the stairs. Clint followed her all the way to her little alcove where the register was kept, and noticed the number of people milling about had definitely dissipated. When she got back behind the front desk and saw that Clint was still there, Anne let out a little surprised noise.

"Oh," she said, shaking her head out of embarrassment. "I didn't know you were still there. With all that's been happening, I seem to be a little distracted."

"That's certainly understandable."

Flipping the page over in her book of guests, Anne ran her finger down the list of names and glanced back up at Clint. "You were mixed up in that fight, weren't you?"

"I do seem to be in the wrong place sometimes."

"Well, at least you weren't hurt." Her head snapped up so she could look at him full on. A worried expression had suddenly overtaken her face. "Were you hurt?"

"No, ma'am," Clint assured her. "But that's kind of you to ask."

Nodding, the older woman looked back down to the book in front of her. "This isn't the quietest place I've ever lived, but there's usually not as much trouble as all this. That Brody and the men that run with him usually bark more than they bite. To tell you the truth, I think lots of folks around here would be just as happy to see them go. I heard that a few of them were shot dead in front of the saloon."

"That's right."

Even though a hint of sadness came across her face, Anne didn't seem half as worried hearing about the loss of Brody's men as she was when she thought Clint might have sustained a scratch. "That's terrible, but what can someone like that expect when they live their life in so much violence?"

"It sounds like this town could use some better law," Clint said.

"Oh, we've tried that plenty of times. Anytime anyone steps up to do more than lock and unlock that smokehouse, Brody or one of his dogs shoots him down. Of course, that's only happened twice, but that's enough to discourage anyone else who might have taken the job."

After hearing all of this, Clint's opinion of Two-Cent Drogan was starting to brighten up a bit. Of course, that all depended on Drogan's reasoning for picking his fight with Brody. Wanting to get rid of a known menace or even going after a reward was one thing. Gunning someone down just for the credit of doing so was another.

Then, there was always the question of why Drogan had been so hot to go after Clint himself.

"Here it is," Anne said, poking her finger on one specific line in the register. "Carlos Granger. He's the man that took that room you were asking about."

"Is he still there?"

Anne's brow furrowed as she replied, "He arrived four days ago. I haven't seen him lately, but I don't have a record of him leaving either. He didn't seem like the sociable type."

"I've bothered you enough, Anne," Clint said with a tip of his hat. "Thanks for all your trouble."

"No trouble at all. Supper will be on the table at five-thirty sharp."

THIRTY-FIVE

Normally, Clint wouldn't have even considered letting someone like Drogan out of his sight. After all the trouble he'd gone through to track the gunfighter this far, Clint's first impulse would have been to stick to Drogan like glue until he figured out what the gunfighter wanted and why there was so much about him that just plain didn't sit right.

But this wasn't a normal situation.

Clint couldn't shake the feeling that there was more to Drogan than just some gunslinger trying to build on his reputation. Two-Cent already had a reputation, and was well past the age where a man like him worried about impressing folks.

On the one hand, he'd killed just to attract attention, as well as to send a message to Clint. On the other hand, the men he'd buried were all killers themselves. The more Clint thought about it, he couldn't recall one instance that he'd heard of Two-Cent Drogan shooting anyone who wasn't also playing the same dangerous game. Clint didn't pretend to know what had happened in every second of Drogan's life, but he did know enough to get a feel for the man's patterns. That was enough to convince any poker player, and it was enough to satisfy Clint's gut that he was right.

One thing his gut was telling him now was that Drogan wasn't finished in Mehlville Crossing. And if he wasn't finished there, the man's patterns were easy enough to read for Clint to know where he could find him. Sure enough, when Clint walked back into that saloon and looked toward the back of the room, he found Drogan sitting alone at one of the tables.

Drogan was staring down at a half-empty bottle when Clint walked up to him. He swirled the whiskey around in his glass as though he was captivated by the potent, rust-colored liquid.

"What the hell is it that you want, Drogan?" Clint asked, knowing damn well that the gunfighter knew he was standing in front of him. "By all accounts, I should be dragging you into a jail cell or avoiding you like the plague just because you're such a pain in my ass."

"Then why don't you pick one and be done with it?" Drogan answered without taking his eyes away from his whiskey.

"Because there's something going on here that I'm missing, and I don't like missing things that go on around me. Especially when that just might cost someone their life."

"Plenty of folks have died around you lately and it doesn't seem to bother you much."

"It's different when someone's drawing down on you and about to put a bullet through your skull. You know that just as much as I do. What you've been doing is charging into fights that you don't think you can win."

"Is that what I'm doing?" Drogan asked sarcastically. "Must be nice to see all and know all. What makes you think I can't win against you or anyone else I choose?"

"What I think doesn't matter. It's what you think." Clint pulled up a chair and sat down across from Drogan.

When he did, he felt as if he was back in Plattsmith. For that matter, they could have been in any saloon in any town at all. Perhaps it was the distant look in Drogan's eyes, or perhaps it was the fact that Clint constantly found himself having conversations with the man in such similar circumstances.

"You're the one that thinks you weren't going to win," Clint continued. "You thought that right outside this place."

"Yeah? And how do you know so much?"

"Because I saw it in your eyes. You were surprised when those men dropped and you didn't. Go on, look me in the eye and tell me different so I can see the lies for myself."

Drogan looked up, took a breath, but dropped his eyes before saying a word. Instead, he let out his breath so slowly that it came from him like steam through a piston as he topped his glass with whiskey from his bottle. "You were a gunsmith, weren't you?" Drogan asked.

Clint was taken aback by the sudden shift in the conversation, but nodded and replied, "Yes. I still practice my trade whenever I get the chance."

"I know they call you The Gunsmith, but that don't make it so in our line of work."

The more Drogan talked, the more it seemed as though he was talking to some ghost living in his whiskey bottle than he was to any flesh-and-blood person sitting right across from him. Clint noticed the glazing in the other man's eyes, and watched Drogan carefully for any more changes in his demeanor.

"What line of work do you think I'm in?" Clint asked.

Drogan shook his head as though he was snapping himself out of a dream and said, "My kind of work. That's what I meant to say, I guess."

"And what is that exactly?"

"I'm a killer, Adams. You knew that already. Everyone

knows that. At least, they used to know that."

And there, in those last couple of words, Clint saw through right down into Luke Drogan's core. Like a flash of a lighthouse's signal through a thick fog, that little bit of perfect truth came through to shine right onto Clint's eyes.

Clint settled into his chair and folded his arms across his chest. When he looked at Drogan this time, he knew exactly what he was searching for. That alone made him feel as though he'd come a hell of a lot farther in the past few seconds than he had in the entire ride from Plattsmith to Mehlville Crossing.

"So what are you now?" Clint asked. "What's so different about you now than it was back in your prime?"

That last part had been a guess on Clint's part as well as a kind of gamble. Fortunately, it was a gamble that wound up paying off.

"Now I'm nothing, Adams. Just another owlhoot in a saloon trying to swim to the bottom of a bottle. I used to be something, though. People used to know who I was and step aside when I walked by." When he looked up this time, Drogan's eyes were perfectly clear and he spoke as though all the whiskey had instantly burned out of his system.

"I'm dying," Drogan said. "And I aim to make sure that Two-Cent is a name that people will remember after I'm gone, and not just what I have in my pocket when they drop me into a box."

THIRTY-SIX

"Dying?"

Of all the things Clint had been expecting to hear, that wasn't on his list. Even though he'd just repeated the word out loud, it still didn't lose its impact.

"You're dying?" Clint asked, even though the grim expression on Drogan's face told him everything he needed to know.

The gunfighter nodded. "Yep. I've heard it from every doctor I've seen, but I think I've known it before anyone ever said it to my face."

Clint had spoken to dying men before. There was a look in their eyes that was unsettling no matter how calloused a man had become. It almost seemed as though men who could see the end to their days reflected that sight when they gazed back at the world.

Some men showed their ailments more than others, whether they tried to hide it or not. Clint had spent time with Doc Holliday himself, and had seen the Reaper in those sunken eyes just as surely as if Death itself was standing behind him. Drogan and Doc were two separate men and two different cases, but now that he knew what

Drogan was dealing with, plenty of other things fit into place.

"So what happened?" Clint asked. "Are you sick? Did you get hurt?"

Drogan shrugged. "Hell if I know. I'm sick, I can tell you that much, but every other doctor I see feeds me a different line of bull. They toss around all kind of fancy words, but it all boils down to the fact that they don't know shit.

"Sometimes I bleed from my nose and sometimes from my mouth. Sometimes I can't sleep and sometimes I can't stand up. My hands are shaky and my eyesight's going bad, but I thought those things were just on account of my advancing years. Toss in the rest and any fool knows there's something wrong besides me just getting old."

"Maybe you should take it easier then."

The look on Drogan's face showed that he was close to laughing at what Clint had just said, but didn't have the strength. "Easier, huh? Just sit back in a sickbed and let the drool run down my face. Is that it?"

Clint couldn't help but think about Doc again. The last time he'd seen him, Holliday had looked like a corpse that somehow found the strength to drape a coat over its shoulders. Even so, asking him to lie back and kick his boots off would have been akin to insulting his mother. The stubborn fire in Doc's eyes was proof enough of that.

Drogan had that fire in his eyes as well, and Clint knew it would be there until the final breath had passed from the old man's lips. Every so often, there was something else in the old man's eyes that dimmed that flame like a momentary shadow. It wasn't enough to douse the flame entirely, but it was enough to show a definite faltering.

No matter how stubborn Drogan may have been, he was still a man, and no man was completely fearless. The shadow that passed quickly through Drogan's mind came and went in the blink of an eye, but was enough to let

Clint know that there was plenty more to see.

"I'm not saying you should give up and crawl away somewhere," Clint told him. "But what's the use of picking fights and putting yourself in even more danger?"

"What's the use? What's the difference is more like it. What the hell difference does it make if I relax or not? I may not know the right words or the proper doctoring phrases to say what's wrong, but I can feel it chewing away at my innards like some bunch of maggots. Some days are better than others, but I know goddamn well I don't have many days left."

"So you'd rather go down fighting. Is that it?"

Drogan looked at Clint and then nodded. "Yeah. If you had the choice, wouldn't you rather have it that way?"

"If I had my choice, I'd rather die with a head full of gray hair in a nice comfortable bed. Not in the middle of some street with a bunch of folks watching like they were at some kind of circus."

"What I do ain't for nobody that's watching, Adams. You should know that more than anybody."

"I don't know what you think of me, but I'm not a gun for hire and I don't kill just to win a fight or prove a point."

Shaking his head, Drogan turned his eyes away from Clint and looked back down into his bottle. "Then maybe I was wrong about you. It wouldn't be the first time I was wrong about somethin', and it sure won't be the last."

The gunfighter lifted his glass and held it under his nose for a moment so he could feel the pungent fumes of the whiskey crawl up into his nose and slide down his throat. "One thing I know I'm not wrong about when it comes to me and you is that we both know what death is truly like." After tossing back the whiskey, Drogan put the glass down and looked up at Clint with that eerie clarity in his eyes.

"We've both killed our share," Drogan said. "And

we've both looked into the faces of dying men when they stop being men and become nothing but slabs of meat. I don't know if I believe in God, but I've seen the face of the devil and I've caught him eyeing me nearly every day of my life."

Clint wanted to tell Drogan that he was wrong once again, but that would be a lie. With all the blood, death, and outright evil he'd seen throughout the years, Clint had to admit he had a face in mind when Drogan mentioned the devil himself. It wasn't anything he could put into words, but it was something he simply understood.

Any man who lived by the gun had seen that dark face every so often either in a drunken haze or in their nightmares.

"So why kill more?" Clint asked. "And why try to kill me? What do you think that will prove?"

"It'll prove that I earned my way in this life and that I wasn't put down by some sickness that makes me cough and wheeze like some goddamn invalid. You and me, we're killers. Whether you do it for money or some cause you believe in, we both carry guns and we both know how to make them weapons sing."

"I've heard about you, Drogan. What you've been doing isn't your style. None of this is. You're acting like some mad-dog kid with a taste for blood. You're better than this."

Drogan leaned back in his chair and swirled what little whiskey remained in his bottle. "Let me tell you a story, Adams. I'm an old man and old men tell stories, so indulge me. Maybe it'll clear something up for you, or maybe it'll give you a little glimpse at what we both got coming for us down the road."

THIRTY-SEVEN

"I was younger back then," Drogan said. Fixing his eyes on Clint, he added, "It's not as clear to me as it could be, but it comes to me every so often like a reminder. Well, maybe more like a nightmare . . ."

It had been a hot summer when it happened. Drogan was a lean, imposing figure with dark hair and eyes that burned with intensity. The copper handle of his gun was shinier than the new penny carved there and he polished it every day. He walked with the confidence of the young and fought with the stupid belief that he could not lose.

Already, he'd killed more men than he wanted to count, and his reputation was big enough to precede him wherever he went. There were always a few men riding with him, but they never stayed with him for very long. Not only was there a constant storm of lead flying around Drogan, but there was enough blood to turn a desert into a crimson swamp. No man could put up with so much death and violence.

Not even the tough ones.

It took a special kind of man to weather a storm like that. It took a man who not only knew he was damned, but didn't mind wallowing in his sins for the rest of his days.

In this particular summer, Drogan had taken up in a small town in Oklahoma. There were a few others riding with him, and they were even starting to plan their next set of robberies, when they heard the old man's voice shrieking at them like a rake on a blackboard.

The old man was a local legend of sorts, and came stumbling into town on shaky legs, wearing tattered buckskins and a beard that was shot through with spit and bramble thorns. He came in waving a rusty pistol and screaming every obscenity he could think of as he made his way down the main street.

"You sons of bitches thought you got rid of me?" the old man screamed. "You cock-sucking prick-eaters think you can just sit there without a goddamn worry in your hollow little heads?"

Drogan had been standing at the bar in the local saloon, nursing a beer and passing the hottest hours in the shade. When he heard those scratchy profanities coming from outside, he looked over to the bartender and asked, "Who the hell is that?"

"I'll be damned," the barkeep said. "That's ol' Kade Daggett. I haven't heard from him in Lord knows how long. Hell, nobody has."

"And who the fuck is Kade Daggett?"

"Used to be a bad man around these parts until the law run him off and he had too many prices on his head to stick his nose out of whatever hole he'd crawled into. Most everyone around here thought he got himself hung somewhere."

"Guess you were wrong." And with that said, Drogan turned back to his drink and kept talking to his partners.

But Kade kept screaming and he kept walking to the saloon. Looking back on it, the older Drogan had to smile and shake his head out of sheer admiration for the old bastard. It almost seemed as though Kade could sniff out the younger gunmen from a mile away.

"I know you're in there, you assholes!" Kade shouted into the saloon. "Get out of my goddamn town!"

Drogan rolled his eyes and ignored the old man. At least, he tried to ignore him. After growing up forced to grit his teeth while being insulted, he didn't have much tolerance left for harsh words being thrown at him. And after killing so many men, he knew he didn't have to grit his teeth through any more if he didn't want to.

Those two things combined to form a nasty mix, which quickly started a fire in Drogan's belly. The fire grew hotter until his fingers clenched around his mug and the muscles in his jaw twitched beneath his skin.

"I know who's in there!" Kade screamed. "Chicken-shit Two-Cent back-shooting son of a bitch!"

Finally, Drogan couldn't take any more. His fist slammed against the bar and he was charging outside before he knew what he was doing. In his mind, it was his father screaming at him, right along with all those kids who'd made his growing-up years a string of one fight after another.

It was what he heard every time he got himself mad enough to kill. It was the trigger for his mind that was every bit as deadly as the one on his gun.

"He's drunk," the barkeep said. "Don't even bother with him. Nobody listens to what he says no more."

But Drogan was too far gone. He could hear the bartender's pleas, but he was a long way from caring about them. When he got outside, all he wanted was to shut that old man's mouth for good and to spill his blood onto the street.

Kade straightened up as best he could. He looked even worse than he sounded, and he stank bad enough for anyone within twenty feet of him to catch his stench in their nostrils.

"I know you all been laughing at me in there," Kade said. "All of that stops right now!"

"I never even heard of you, old man," Drogan shot back.

When he heard that, Kade flinched as though he'd been struck, and his mouth twisted and turned as if he wanted more than anything to say something, but just couldn't find the words. "Yeah?" he grunted after an uncomfortable amount of time had passed. "We'll just see about that."

Drogan wasn't about to let anyone talk to him like that. He didn't even want folks looking at him the way the petulant old man was doing just then. He'd put up with it more than enough already, and was never going to do it again.

The final straw was when Kade hacked up a mouthful of phlegm and spat it on the ground at Drogan's feet. After that, even the shred of pity Drogan felt wasn't enough to keep him from drawing his gun.

Without another word, Drogan's hand flashed down to his side and plucked the copper-handled .44 out of its holster. He brought up the gun and thumbed the hammer back in one smooth motion, aiming from the hip.

To the older man's credit, he got hold of the pistol wedged in his chewed-up belt, and nearly got it free by the time Drogan's weapon was drawn. The end of the barrel stuck beneath his belt, however, and kept him from pulling the gun free.

Desperation flooded the old man's face as he tried over and over to pull out his gun and defend himself. His hands flapped against the side of the weapon, tugging at it until even his ragged pants shook with each panicked attempt.

Drogan stood there with his finger tensed around his trigger, but stopping short of dropping the hammer. He watched Kade's draw as it became more and more flustered, until it finally became pathetic. The more Kade tugged at that gun stuck under his belt, the funnier the sight became. Once the tension was completely gone from the situation, the people who'd gathered around to watch a fight instead laughed at the spectacle the conflict had become.

Standing there with his gun still aimed at Kade's heart, Drogan felt a smile form on his face and a laugh rumble up from his belly. Before too long, he holstered his gun and laughed right along with the rest of the crowd.

Kade managed to yank his gun free, which caused a few people to laugh harder and the rest to start applauding, whooping, and hollering. The old man tried to snarl and cuss, but all he got was more laughs and more applause.

Finally, holding his weapon in a limp hand, Kade fixed his eyes on Drogan and said, "Why couldn't you let me die like a man?"

Kade then pressed the barrel of his gun underneath his stubbly chin and pulled the trigger . . .

THIRTY-EIGHT

Clint watched as Drogan finished his story. The changes in the older man's face had been remarkable. At first, he'd seemed nostalgic. Then, he'd become reflective, before some of that anger from all that time ago came rushing back to flush his cheeks and gnash his teeth together.

When he'd talked about Kade trying again and again to draw his gun, Drogan had even gotten Clint to crack a smile.

And when he mentioned Kade blowing his own head off, Drogan's eyes glazed over and he reflexively took another pull from his bottle.

"I never saw nothing like it," Drogan said once the liquor had washed down his throat. "I mean, I've seen men shot and I've even seen men hurt worse than that old man Kade. I once turned a fella's head into red smoke using a shotgun, but that didn't stick with me like seeing Kade shoot himself like that.

"Somehow, it struck me as cruel. The way he just looked at me, said those words, and then . . ." He let his sentence trail off while slowly shaking his head. "I can still smell the dirt on that old man's clothes and the piss that ran down his leg when he stopped twitching. Some

155

of those bastards standing nearby laughed at that too. Those godless pricks."

Drogan looked up at Clint, who had yet to say anything now that the story had been completed. "You see it, don't you, Adams? You see what waits for both of us if we don't play our cards right?"

"You're worried about becoming like Kade?" Clint asked.

"Like him? I'm already like him. I think about that old man's face and I see a wolf that lived long enough to watch his teeth fall from his head. And a wolf without his teeth is like a gunfighter who's getting too damn old to draw his weapon and do what he was born to do."

"But you can still draw. I've seen you. You don't need to prove anything because you don't need to turn into that old man."

When Drogan thought about what Clint told him, his mouth curled a bit as though he'd tasted something that had gone bad. "I won't turn into that old man, that's for damn sure. I'll see to it that I give folks something more to remember me by than a rusty gun and a stinking corpse."

"There's more to it than that," Clint insisted. "I've seen the men you go after. Well, apart from me, they're men that would be hunted down by the law anyway. I've already heard enough about Brody and his crew to know that you were doing this whole town a favor by taking them down a notch."

Smirking at that, Drogan said, "They jumped me the moment I first rode in here a few weeks ago. They were itching to kill anyone just for the hell of it. You know the type."

"Yeah. I do. And I also know that this place needed someone like you to stand up to them. Isn't that how you'd rather be remembered?"

"Brody don't have more than a man or two left to follow him."

"You say that like it's a bad thing."

"It isn't. Not yet. There's enough left for him to do what I need him to do."

"And what's that?" Clint asked.

Before he answered, Drogan stared at Clint and swirled the whiskey in his bottle back and forth. Instead of responding to the question, he said, "Old Man Kade is how any man like us winds up when he loses the respect that he's built up over an entire lifetime. I swore on the day Kade shot himself that I wouldn't wind up like him. I'd make sure I kept the respect I'd earned and never let anyone put me down again."

"Even if it meant you had to cheat?"

That stopped Drogan cold in his tracks. The shock on his face came and went in a blink, but it was as obvious as a flash of lightning because Clint had been watching for that very thing.

"What the hell do you mean by that?" Drogan snarled.

Clint shrugged and leaned back in his chair, but made sure not to let his eyes stray from Drogan for an instant. "It seems to me that the thought of that poor old man tugging at his gun like a fool would stick with you for a long time."

"I already told you that much."

"It would stick with you when you're thinking about getting old yourself," Clint went on, ignoring the increasingly hostile look on Drogan's face. "It might even stick with you enough that you feel your own hand start to shake at the wrong moment, especially if you haven't downed your bottle of whiskey for the day.

"My guess is that it would have started coming back to you long before now." Clint leaned forward slightly and lowered his voice just enough so that Drogan listened to him even more. "I'll bet you already tripped up once.

Maybe even came close to getting yourself killed by some punk kid who's got no business taking out the likes of Two-Cent Drogan.

"Did you miss your draw one time, Luke? Did you feel your gun catch on your holster and start to hear those people laughing the way they did all that time ago?"

Drogan's eyes were wide and his normal expression peeled away to reveal a mask of frightened hatred. "Shut up," he said, giving Clint a hint of what he might have sounded like when he was a scared little kid being picked on by local bullies.

"Did you almost miss your draw or maybe even lose some fight in a bar somewhere that made you wonder if others saw you as some sorry old man trying to talk tough and walk tall?"

"I said shut up, goddamn you."

But Clint didn't even flinch. Instead, he kept right on talking in the same level tone of voice. "Did you barely make it out of some scrape that you would have coasted through in your younger days and realize that you're actually slowing down with age? And when that happened, did you decide to regain some of that glory by making sure you never lost another fight, even if it meant hiring someone to hang back with a rifle and pick off your targets over your shoulder from a distance?"

"You don't know what it's like, Adams."

"Sure I do. I've seen plenty of men like you come and go. The thing is that most of them go long before they get old, don't they? The lawmen can find work somewhere else, but the killers and thieves don't retire, do they?"

"I thought you'd understand," Drogan said through clenched teeth.

"I think I understand it perfectly. I'm not guessing here. I know for a fact you've got someone working with you, and it seems to me that they're working even better than you wanted them to."

"Just wait and you'll find out for yourself, Adams. Wait till you start feeling like a goddamn piece of garbage. Just wait till people start laughing at you behind your back."

"Why were you so shocked when those men started dropping in the street?" Clint asked, ignoring what had come from Drogan's mouth before. "Was that not part of the deal? Was your sniper supposed to leave someone behind to finish you off?"

"No," Drogan snapped, sweeping his bottle onto the floor using the flat of his hand. "That's your job."

The gunfighter had spoken in a voice that was barely more than a whisper, but it struck Clint like a clap of thunder.

"If you want me to reform, you're dumber than you look," Drogan sneered. "If you want me to retire, you'll have to retire me. And if you want me to stop coming after you, you'll have to put me into the fucking ground. You got that, Adams?"

Clint didn't answer. He knew anything he said would be lost within the swirl of anger churning inside Drogan's head.

The older man pushed away from the table and practically jumped to his feet. "I don't care if you've listened to me or not. Just be ready because the next time I see you, only one of us is walking away."

Drogan stormed out of the saloon. Anyone who'd been watching the argument couldn't move fast enough to get out of his way.

THIRTY-NINE

Clint knew better than to try and follow Drogan at that point. The older man was already hot under the collar, and chasing him down would have just made the situation worse. So rather than make any move at all, Clint simply sat back and listened to the other man's footsteps clomp out of the saloon.

As he listened, Clint was also waiting for Two-Cent to stop, turn around, and possibly even take a shot at him right then and there. He'd seen plenty of fire in Drogan's eyes, and could feel the violence boiling to the surface as the conversation had been pushed further and further.

But the shot never came, and Drogan kept right on walking until the saloon doors banged shut behind him. After he was gone, there was a chilling silence hanging in the air. Clint could feel the eyes upon him as every last person in the saloon waited for him to make his move.

At that moment, Clint got a genuine taste for what had driven a man like Drogan into so many gunfights. Despite the fact that they were just a bunch of locals gathered in a saloon hoping to see some blood get spilled, the excitement was thick in the air and Clint could feel it coursing through him.

Clint was no stranger to gunmen earning their reputations, but it had been some time since he'd felt so squarely on display. When he looked around at the faces nearby, Clint saw each one of them turn away from him as if they were all afraid he might turn on them next. That suited Clint just fine and after a minute or two, he walked out of the saloon and into the refreshing cold.

For the first time since he'd arrived in Mehlville Crossing, Clint got the feeling that Drogan might try to cut and run. The older man had gotten his fights and had made his show, so he might just want to move on no matter what he'd said to Clint earlier.

As skilled as he was at reading people, Clint couldn't say for sure whether Drogan meant to follow through on his twisted brand of retirement now or later. His eyes had showed staunch conviction, but his temperament wasn't nearly so easy to read. By Clint's estimation, Two-Cent could just as likely have been riding out of town or picking his spot for a showdown at that very moment.

The only way to know for sure was to wait and see.

Unfortunately, Clint wasn't very good at simply waiting. Although he couldn't predict every last thing Drogan might do, Clint knew for certain that the older man was dangerous and unpredictable. With that combination, someone always got hurt. At least so far, the only ones to get hurt had been the ones who deserved to be on that road in the first place.

The afternoon slipped away into evening as Clint made his rounds about town looking for Drogan. What surprised him was the fact that he was unable to locate the older man after several hours of asking around and looking for himself.

It was a small town, to be sure, but even he wasn't able to poke his nose into every room of every building in that amount of time. As for the locals he talked to, they'd all seen enough of Drogan in action to lose their anxiousness to do anything that might put them on his bad side. Rather than try to push anyone farther than they wanted to go, Clint merely thanked them for their time and went on his way.

At the end of the day, he wound up right back where he'd started: in the stable across from Anne's hotel. Eclipse was alone with that petulant mule inside the drafty building, and the smell of smoke still hung in the air. Every breeze that came along howled through the cracks in the walls and stirred up stray bits of dust and straw.

Clint reached out to pat the Darley Arabian's snout, and could feel the stallion's anxiousness to get out of his stall.

"You want to get out of here, boy? I can't say as I blame you."

At that moment, Clint seriously considered ditching the town himself. The very thought of saddling up Eclipse and riding away seemed especially good after the trials he'd faced in dealing with the likes of Brody and Drogan. But there was still much to be done in Mehlville Crossing, and Clint just couldn't bear the thought of leaving too many loose ends behind him.

That little fault had given him plenty of sleepless nights and gotten him into more scrapes than he could count.

But it was that same fault that let him sleep at night rather than be plagued by the demons that pushed a man like Luke Drogan to the brink of suicide. All in all, Clint figured he got the better end of that bargain.

FORTY

"Looking for some company?"

The voice echoed through the stable as the sound of the door being pushed open was still rumbling through the air. Clint had heard the first sound of the door moving, and was watching that part of the building out of the corner of his eye. He recognized the shape of the figure entering the stable even before hearing the familiar voice.

"That would be nice, Megan," Clint said, looking over toward the shapely brunette who walked closer to him. "Eclipse here is one of a kind, but he's not much for conversation."

Megan walked up to stand beside Clint, and leaned slightly against the stall. Reaching out with both hands, she rubbed the Darley Arabian's muzzle and smiled warmly. "He's beautiful. Looks like he's got plenty of spirit too."

"You can say that again. In fact, you'd better not. If he gets wind that we're talking about anything close to him going out for a run, he might just kick a wall down."

Megan laughed and kept stroking the white spot on Eclipse's nose. Her long, articulate fingers traced easy

163

lines along the horse's skin, calming the stallion until he
looked about ready to lay down for a nap.

Clint watched her as she went through the simple motions. Her long hair was pulled back into a single braid
without one strand falling over her face. The skin of her
cheeks was smooth as ivory, and her wide hazel eyes were
clear as crystal.

Her full pink lips curled into a smile as she turned to
look at him. Standing that close, Clint realized just how
tall and slender she truly was. Her eyes were on the same
level as his, yet she didn't hold herself in the way that
most taller women did. Unlike those others, Megan wasn't
about to apologize for her bearing either through words
or her actions.

"I hear you've had a busy day," Megan said, her
smooth, soft voice drifting through the cold air.

Thinking about the day he had was almost enough to
break the tranquility that had fallen over Clint. Almost,
but not quite.

"You heard about all that, huh?" Clint asked.

Megan smirked even wider, and shifted her weight so
her hip was leaning against the front of Eclipse's stall.
"Just about everyone in town's heard about it. The rest of
them actually saw it."

"Good Lord," Clint said, rolling his eyes. "I guess
that's one reason why I'm glad ol' Eclipse here can't
talk."

"I guess you've probably already heard more than your
fill about everything that went on."

"And then some."

"That's just the burden of being the talk of the town,
huh?"

Megan reached out to run her fingers gently along
Clint's chin. At that moment, he got a real good sense of
what was going on in the stallion's mind when she was
stroking his hair and nearly lulling him to sleep. Her touch

was soothing, and made Clint's mind drift away from the many things that had been bothering him.

After a couple of seconds, he let his eyes close slightly. It was only for half a second or so, but when he opened them again, Clint was greeted by the sight of Megan's face drifting closer to his own. She was even more beautiful at that closer distance, and he found himself anticipating the touch of her soft, full lips.

She kissed him gently, but let the moment linger on for long enough to get a reaction from Clint's entire body. Just when it felt as if she was going to pull away, Megan let out a little moan and slid her fingers along the back of Clint's neck and up into his hair. Without breaking contact, her lips pressed against him a little harder and she moved her body so her breasts pushed against Clint's chest.

Clint let his instincts take over and allowed his hands to wander freely over Megan's body. She didn't make a single move to stop him, and writhed just enough to guide his hands to even better places. It seemed at first as though time had slowed down from the moment Clint got a taste of Megan's lips. Then as their kiss became deeper and more passionate, time seemed to stop altogether.

Feeling the smooth curves of her body beneath his hands, Clint didn't much care about anything else that was going on in the world at that moment. Considering what was waiting for him out there, he didn't mind missing out on some of it one bit. He was perfectly content sharing the warmth of her body and listening to the contented little noises that Megan made as her tongue traced gently over his lips.

Clint didn't know how much time had passed, but was aware the instant she broke away from him. Moving just her head, Megan pulled in a slow breath and locked her hands behind his neck.

"I hope you don't mind if I'm a little forward," she said.

Clint smiled and brushed his lips against her earlobe so she could just hear him when he whispered, "The only thing I mind is that you stopped."

He could feel her body melting even closer against him as she allowed herself to be pulled in even tighter within Clint's arms. Even with the close proximity of their bodies, Megan still managed to lean back just enough to tug apart the top couple of buttons on her shirt.

"Believe me," she said. "Stopping is the last thing on my mind right now."

Clint looked down and watched as she pulled apart the two upper halves of her shirt. The tops of her breasts were smooth and luminescent in the faltering light within the stable. Beneath the shirt, she wore a simple white camisole with a hint of lace around the upper edge. He helped her pull the shirt open by peeling it apart himself, and when he ran his hands over the gentle swell of her breasts, Clint found her nipples to be small and completely erect.

As she felt his hands move over her body, Megan let out moaning little breaths that became louder and more drawn out the more Clint touched her. When she felt his hands come down to cup her buttocks and lift her off her feet, she wrapped her legs around him and leaned in to begin nibbling his neck.

She didn't care where he was taking her. All she wanted was to feel more of the promising bulge between his legs.

FORTY-ONE

Clint carried her deeper into the stable, where there were a few empty stalls and several piles of straw. He stepped right over the charred remains of the fire he'd started the previous night, and didn't once think about the fight that he'd had within those same four walls. Instead, the only thing going through his mind was the feel of Megan's body and the smell of her skin pressed so close to his own.

She was still nibbling on his neck when she felt herself being lowered down onto the biggest pile of hay. The feeling of being taken completely off her feet and just put down wherever Clint pleased brought an excitement to her entire body. By the time she felt her back settle into the straw, she was even more eager to get out of her clothes and get Clint inside her.

When he dropped down onto the floor, Clint was already pulling open his shirt and unbuckling his gun belt. The Colt landed heavily onto the floor along with Megan's boots and a good portion of her clothes. Having stripped off everything but her camisole Megan began helping tear away Clint's clothes as well.

He was too eager to let himself be undressed com-

pletely. Under different circumstances, Clint might have
enjoyed removing Megan's clothing piece by piece. As it
was, however, it was all he could do to keep himself from
ripping the material in half as he pulled aside both her
clothes and his own.

Although he pulled open his jeans and started to take
them down, it was Megan who practically ripped them off
him so she could reach down to wrap her hand around
his hard cock. Her touch was eager and just strong enough
to take Clint's breath away without being too rough.

Clint moved his hand between her thighs and felt the
hot dampness waiting for him there. When his thumb
brushed against the sensitive nub of her clit, he watched
as Megan pulled in a quick breath and arched her back
against the floor.

"You like that, huh?" he whispered.

She was beyond the ability to form words, but responded by spreading her legs open for him even more.
The moment one of Clint's fingertips eased between the
lips of her vagina, Megan groaned and started to slowly
pump her hips against his hand.

Looking down at her, watching the pleasure show itself
all over her face, Clint smiled and kept massaging her
soft, moist flesh. "You do like that. Here," he said, moving himself down so he could lower his mouth directly
onto her pussy. "Let's see how you like this."

Before she realized that he'd shifted position, Megan
felt Clint's breath between her legs and his tongue flick
over her slick vagina. Her eyes shot open and she reached
down to grab the back of Clint's head with both hands.

"Oh, yes," she whispered. When Clint slid his tongue
over her clit and then down the entire length of her wet,
pink lips, she felt her breath catch in her throat and her
fingers hold him right where he was.

"Yes! Jesus, don't stop," she moaned.

Clint didn't have any intention of stopping. On the

contrary, he was savoring the taste of her as she got wetter and wetter against his mouth. Her legs tightened around him, and all he had to do was slip the tip of his tongue inside her and Megan would pump her hips forward with a little cry of ecstasy.

Before too long, Clint couldn't hold out any longer. As much pleasure as he got from driving Megan crazy with his tongue, his erection was so hard that it would only start to hurt if he didn't get inside her. He was nowhere close to hurting when he moved up and settled in between her thighs, the warm wetness of her pussy soothing the anxious fire inside him.

Megan's eyes were clenched shut and she turned her head as though she was already caught up in a rapture. The rest of her body acted of its own accord, and she shifted beneath him so all he needed to do was push his hips forward to enter her.

It felt as though he'd been waiting for weeks to feel her body envelop him like that. The warmth of her flesh wrapped tightly around his cock and took every inch of him as he eased all the way inside her. Clint supported himself with both hands against the floor, and found himself grabbing fistfuls of straw as he began pumping in and out between her legs.

Megan forced herself to take a deep breath, and when she opened her eyes, she smiled widely at Clint. From there, she moved just the right way every now and then to make the pleasure that much more intense for both of them.

After burying his cock inside her, Clint leaned his face down so he could run his tongue along her body. From that angle, he could just get his mouth between the upper half of her breasts, but he savored every last bit of the flesh there. She was sweet and just a little salty. Her nipples were rigid, and she shuddered slightly as he tickled them with his tongue.

Clint moved his mouth up again, tracing a slow line toward her neck. He froze like a deer caught at the wrong end of a hunter's rifle when he heard the main doors of the stable rumble open and at least two sets of feet step inside.

"Anyone in here?" came a voice that was completely unfamiliar to Clint.

Megan's eyes were wide as she looked up at Clint like a young girl who'd been caught out after dark. When she felt Clint start to move back so he could get to his gun and clothes, she tightened her legs around him and lifted her hips to keep him inside.

As much as he didn't like getting caught with his pants down, Clint wouldn't have been able to leave her when she moved like that even if the stable caught on fire again. So instead, he lowered himself down so his body was once again pressed tightly against Megan's.

From there, she wrapped her legs even tighter around him until she could lock her ankles at the small of his back.

"I swear I saw someone come in here," grumbled one of the men who had stuck their noses into the stable.

"Can't be too careful around here, that's for sure," said the other. "Not with all that's been happening."

Both sets of footsteps got closer, and Clint felt his entire body start to tense. He could feel Megan tensing as well, but that only made him want to stay right where he was no matter who was about to walk right up and find them.

As the footsteps drew even closer, Megan's smile widened and she started shifting her hips up and down. Her eyes darted between Clint and the men approaching the stall. The more subtle the moves she made, the harder Clint became inside her. She even had to concentrate to keep from making a noise as his erection brushed against a spot that sent the first shiver of an orgasm beneath her skin.

The footsteps stopped a matter of inches before either of the two men would have been close enough to peek into Clint and Megan's stall to catch them in the hay.

"Aw, to hell with this," the first man said. "There ain't nothin' in here but the horses."

"Yeah. It's too damn cold for anything to last long in here anyhow."

And with that, both men stomped away from the back stall and left the stable entirely.

Megan smiled and rubbed her foot against Clint's back. "That's funny. It sure doesn't feel cold where I'm at."

"No," Clint said, resuming his thrusting rhythm between her legs. "It sure doesn't."

FORTY-TWO

Clint and Megan had gone back into the hotel so they could get all the hay off each other in Clint's room. They'd wound up spending another hour or so getting dirty, but only in the sense that a man and woman could get dirty between the sheets. After that, Clint had gone to stretch his legs, and had just returned to find Megan buttoning up her shirt.

"I heard you and some other gunfighter in town nearly started shooting each other in the saloon," Megan said after Clint stepped back into the room.

"You heard about that, huh?" Clint asked. "Word does travel fast around here."

"It's a small town."

"Then I'm surprised nobody else has figured out that Drogan doesn't even do his own shooting."

"What?"

Clint glanced over at her and nodded. "That's right. He's got someone with a rifle picking off his targets from a distance. You ask me, that's not even necessary since he could do just fine on his own."

Megan looked surprised, but Clint watched her face from the corner of his eye.

"That's odd," was all she said.

"I know. It just surprises me that someone like Two-Cent Drogan would need to hire some gutless back-shooter when he can just as well put his man down face-to-face."

Megan nodded and started pulling on her boots. Her feet slapped into each one with a loud thump as she pulled it on.

"Whoever that man is with the rifle," Clint continued, "it sure seems to me that Drogan is wasting his money on him."

"Really? Why's that?"

"Because a seasoned gunfighter like him doesn't need any sort of edge. Especially from some punk kid who thinks his shit don't stink just because he can shoot some-one outside of pistol range." Clint paused and let out a few short laughs. "I'll even bet the man behind that rifle thinks he's pretty tough, when the truth is that he's too yellow to step up and put his life on the line.

"You probably don't know what I'm talking about, but it takes a real man to face someone down like that. But shooting someone with a rifle? That takes as much guts as it would to kill some squirrel or knock a can off a fence post."

Both of Megan's feet hit the floor and she pushed away from the bed with enough force to scoot the whole thing over half an inch. "I've got to go," she said sharply.

Clint watched her with a puzzled expression. "What's the matter?"

When she turned around, she looked at him with a smile and stepped up to place both hands on his face. "Just some things I need to settle, and then"—she paused so she could plant a kiss on him that was both passionate and intense at the same time—"I'm all yours."

"Well, if you can't find me when you get back don't worry. I've got some business of my own to handle."

"What business is that, Clint?"

"I'm going to find that gutless coward behind Drogan's rifle and put him out of his misery. That way I can face down Two-Cent without having some asshole step in un-invited."

With that, Megan's smile dropped away like wet paint sliding off a slick wall. Her eyes narrowed and the lips that had just been kissing him now parted to show a thin line of clenched teeth.

"You think facing Two-Cent Drogan would be any challenge?" Megan asked. When she spoke the other man's name, she spit out the words as though they tasted like sour milk. "That old man should consider himself lucky that he's got someone watching his back. I'd say the person behind that rifle is more dangerous than five Luke Drogans."

Footsteps were sounding in the hall, and although Clint heard them, he figured they could just as well be Anne and one of her helpers coming to investigate the sudden rise in Megan's voice.

"Why are you coming to that gutless bastard's de-fense?" Clint asked, making sure to put a smug tone in his voice. "He won't need it since his worthless hide will be stretched out on a barn door by morning."

"What makes you so sure of that? What makes you so goddamn special?"

"Because I know what I'm dealing with. More impor-tantly, I know who I'm dealing with."

Those footsteps were still coming. They were getting louder by the second, telling Clint that whoever was mak-ing them was a whole lot bigger than Anne.

"Why are you so worked up over this, Megan? Afraid I might not walk out onto that street again and put my back to that lovely window of yours?"

Megan took a step back and fixed her eyes on Clint with a hateful stare. "What are you talking about?"

"Drop the innocent act," Clint said. "I was buying it for too long, but I'm not anymore."

"Anne told me you were in my room. I should be the one that's suspicious of you. Besides, didn't you get a good enough look in there to know I don't even have a gun? All you had to do was ask and I would've—"

"You would've what?" Clint interrupted. "Hidden that Sharps rifle of yours underneath that floorboard under the bottom left bedpost?"

Megan's words caught in her throat.

Nodding, Clint leaned in closer to her and showed her the ace he'd been hiding up his sleeve. "I got a good look the first time, but I got a much better look the second. You're thinking about that walk I took a few minutes ago, aren't you? Well, you should be. That's when I got into your room and took a closer look for myself. I would've thought you'd have more practice at pulling up floorboards. That one you took up in your room wasn't as neat as I might expect from a professional. But you're not a professional, are you?"

"I'm ten times the gunman that Drogan ever was."

Clint nodded as the hairs rose up on the back of his neck. Those footsteps had stopped close by, but he'd broken through Megan's shell and wasn't about to turn back now.

"I don't know how you and Drogan hooked up," Clint said. "But my guess is that you got a taste for killing just like he does. Just like every other gunfighter who realized that they were awful good at some awful bad things."

"What do you know about it? You don't know me!"

"I know what I saw. I know the look of surprise on Drogan's face when more men than he wanted were shot dead right in front of him. He tried to cover it up, but you got carried away, didn't you? That taste for killing was just a little too good to stop when you were supposed to, wasn't it?"

The rage in Megan's eyes burned brighter for a moment, but was soon brought back down to a manageable flicker. When she spoke this time, her tone was careful and measured. It was the voice of a cold-blooded murderer.

"So what now, Clint Adams? You think you can just shoot me? You don't have it in you."

"You're playing a dangerous game, Megan. You need to fold before you lose everything you've got."

She waited for a second before smirking and whispering, "Fuck you." Then, from out of nowhere, she opened her mouth and let out a shout that roared through the room and beyond. "Now!"

The footsteps thundered right outside the door, a woman shrieked from another part of the hotel, men burst into the room, and all hell was set loose.

FORTY-THREE

Clint saw everything unfold slowly. As soon as he saw the fight coming for him, he paid such close attention to everything that the men rushing him now seemed to be coming a little slower. Although it helped him make sense of all the chaos around him, that didn't mean he was in any less danger.

Right away, Clint saw that the men charging into the room had their guns drawn and were bringing them to bear on him. He reacted without having to think, twisting his body around while pulling his Colt free of its holster. The modified iron filled his hand as though it was a part of him, and he aimed from the hip while his finger was already squeezing the trigger.

As if the sound of raised voices and pounding footsteps wasn't enough, the roar of gunfire turned everything else into a jarring mess. Smoke and sparks filled the air as Clint's gun threw hot lead toward the door.

The other men fired as well, but their shots came more out of panic. One of the men fired straight into the floor, while the one in the lead took a nip out of Clint's leg.

Clint felt the bite of the bullet as it grazed his thigh, knowing instantly that it wasn't anything to worry about.

The man he'd been shooting at, on the other hand, wasn't nearly as lucky. Clint watched as that one's chest was drilled by the Colt's first round, dropping the man at the front of the charge like a rock.

That first gunman's eyes were glazing over before his back hit the floor, but that didn't stop the one behind him from adjusting his aim so he could get a better angle on Clint.

Just as Clint was shifting his hand to prepare for his second shot, something bumped him from behind so hard that it forced him to blast a hole through the wall by the door. That bump came from Megan as she pushed him aside so she could run past him and into the hallway. The only thing preventing that second gunman from taking full advantage of the distraction was that Megan had to shove him aside as well in order for her to escape the room.

Even with the woman charging past them both, that gunman's shot hissed through the air disturbingly close to Clint's face. He didn't have time to be rattled by the near miss, so he took a third shot as if nothing had happened.

That was one of the tricks of surviving a gunfight. If a man could keep his head and think about what needed to be done instead of what might happen, he was already miles ahead of most others, who simply let themselves get pissed enough to pull their gun.

That trick saved Clint's life, while ending the life of that second gunman as a well-aimed round tore a messy hole through the center of his forehead. Still clutching his gun and wearing a strange look of surprise on his face, the second man dropped first to his knees, and then flopped onto his face.

Clint was already bounding through the door before the second man started to twitch. Although he knew he had to be careful entering that hall, he also knew that Anne was in some very unpleasant company at the moment. There was still hope for her, however, because it sounded as though she was still healthy enough to put up a fight.

"Let go of me!" the older woman screamed. "What's going on here? What do you want?"

There was nobody else in the hall, and Clint met no other resistance before making it to the top of the stairs.

"Shut the hell up, bitch!"

That voice was definitely Brody's. Hearing it only made Clint take the stairs two at a time on his way down. No matter how much he hurried, Clint still wasn't fast enough to get down the stairs before Brody had dragged the older woman outside through the front door.

Brody was still dragging her roughly away from the hotel as Clint came charging outside. A shot cracked through the air as Brody squeezed off a round toward the first sign of movement he spotted emerging from the building. Having anticipated that very thing, Clint was keeping his head down, and moved off to one side the instant he'd cleared the door frame.

It didn't matter to Clint how close that shot came. All that mattered was that it didn't hit him and Anne was still in trouble.

"Let her go, Brody," Clint shouted.

The other man dragged her further into the street, and didn't stop until he'd put plenty of space between himself and Clint and the hotel. As he spun around to face Clint, Brody couldn't decide if he wanted to aim his gun at him or keep it pressed against Anne's temple.

"Not another step," Brody said. "Hold it right there or this old bat gets it." With that, he wedged the barrel of his gun against Anne's skull and held it there.

Clint watched him carefully, measuring the level of desperation in his eyes. The closer Clint looked, the more tension he could feel, until Clint's nerves were jangling in time with the frenzy that must have been going through both Anne and Brody's minds.

"Let her go and this can end up without anyone getting hurt," Clint warned. "You pull that trigger and I'll make sure you die before your ears stop ringing."

Brody started shaking his head. It was slow at first, but gathered momentum as his eyes got wider and wider. Then, he made one of those slips that was small enough by itself, but monumental considering that it had been precisely what Clint had been waiting for.

Brody's eyes had been snapping from Clint to Anne and back again, until they jumped up to look over Clint's head at the hotel behind him. When Brody looked back, he had the arrogance of a man who thought he held all the cards and his mouth formed a grim, determined line as he tightened his finger around his trigger.

Clint adjusted his aim in a fraction of a second and fired. The bullet whipped through the air and blew a messy chunk out of Brody's shoulder. The impact was enough to pull his gun hand away from Anne's head just long enough for Clint to send another round through his left eye. As he fell, Brody's finger clenched and he sent a shot straight up into the sky.

As soon as Brody stumbled backward, Anne dashed away from him. The old woman was shaken up, but otherwise unharmed. Clint then spun around on the balls of his feet to see what Brody had been looking at in the moment before those last fatal shots had been fired.

As Clint had suspected, Megan was leaning out her window, sighting along the barrel of her rifle. When he'd checked out her room earlier, Clint had taken the time to empty the weapon. In the next second, he saw Megan slide a fresh round into the breech with a quick, practiced hand. The new round was levered in and she was ready to fire by the time Clint had twisted his body around and started bringing his hand up to point the Colt in her direction.

It was at that moment that he realized he might not be

fast enough to get the drop on the skilled and experienced sniper. He knew he could take a shot, but it would be rushed. Unfortunately, he had no choice but to hurry and just pull his trigger before Megan took the shot she'd been lining up ever since Clint had followed Brody into the street.

When Clint heard the gunshot blast through the air, he knew it hadn't come from his Colt. He also knew it might very well be the last thing he would ever hear.

FORTY-FOUR

The shot came before Clint could pull his trigger, but it did not come from Megan's rifle. Instead, the bullet came from behind Clint, passed over his head, and punched a neat little hole through Megan's chest.

Feeling the fatal wound, but not quite able to believe that she was truly about to die, Megan dropped her rifle and slumped back into her room.

Clint spun around on his heels with his gun raised, his finger still less than a hairbreadth from pulling the trigger. He was greeted by the sight of a lone figure standing in the street with a smoking gun in his hand.

"Drogan?" Clint said with genuine surprise.

Two-Cent nodded and slowly placed his .44 into its holster. "This is between just you and me now. My choice still stands. You retire me here and now in front of all these people or you die where you stand."

"Isn't there anything else you can do with your life besides throw it away?"

"There is, but I'm a gunfighter. We ain't supposed to get to be my age anyhow. I could raise horses, but I'll always know I got unfinished business or that some other kid will come hunt me down to make their own name mean something."

"You're a changed man, Drogan. You've proven that."

But Two-Cent's eyes were cold and set firmly on the path he'd chosen for himself. "I'll let you reload and then we finish this."

Clint flipped open the Colt's cylinder and exchanged the spent shells for fresh ones. "So you either want to kill me or die?" Clint asked while snapping the pistol shut with a flick of his wrist.

"Yep. Either way, I win."

Knowing that Drogan was too far along to be talked out of anything now, Clint holstered his gun and squared off with the other man. "This is your show, Two-Cent. You start it."

Drogan pulled in a deep breath, savoring every last bit of it. He thought back to the moments in his life, all of them leading up to this very moment. All in all, he was happy with the way things had turned out. Having started out as the kid everyone pushed around and shoved aside, then growing into a man everyone feared, he was now poised to be a man everyone respected.

Even though he knew he had a better chance of talking a bull out of its horns, Drogan figured that killing The Gunsmith would be the ultimate accomplishment for a man in his line of work.

And as for being gunned down by Clint Adams after facing him with his chin held high, well, there sure wasn't any shame in that.

Letting out the breath he'd been holding, Drogan reached for his gun knowing damn well that it would be the last time he would ever do it again.

Clint's eyes were steady and he waited for the first sign of motion from the other man's gun arm. When that sign came, he snatched the Colt from his hip with the speed

and ease of a well-oiled machine that had only been built
for one purpose.

Even Drogan was impressed.

The Colt barked once and sent a round into Drogan
that filled the air with a spray of blood. The Colt then
barked again, again, again, and again, until all but one of
Clint's bullets had been expended. When the shooting
stopped, the air was filled with smoke and it seemed as
though a violent storm had just blown through town.

The copper-plated .44 hit the dirt and Drogan followed
soon after. The old man dropped to his knees and opened
his mouth, but was in too much pain to make a sound.
Even though he was getting dizzy and lightheaded, he
could still see Clint walking straight toward him.

Clint stopped, looked around at the crowd that had
gathered, and squatted down to Drogan's level. Both men
looked down at Two-Cent's wounds. All five bullets had
taken out chunks of Drogan's hands, with one shot even
snipping off the top of his trigger finger cleaner than a
surgeon could have done the job. The wounds were far
from fatal, but Drogan would never be able to draw a gun
again.

When Clint looked into Drogan's eyes, he said, "You
can still raise horses with those hands."

Still dizzy from the pain and shock, Drogan nodded.
"My gun," he said. "Take it."

Clint looked over at the masterfully crafted weapon.
"Are you sure about that?"

"Yeah. I'm retired."

Watch for

GUILTY AS CHARGED

274th novel in the exciting GUNSMITH
series from Jove

Coming in October!

J. R. ROBERTS

THE GUNSMITH

LONGARM

Explore the exciting Old West with one of the men who made it wild!